the girls

the ✶Girls

story by

Amy Goldman Koss

SCHOLASTIC INC.

New York Toronto London Auckland Sydney
Mexico City New Delhi Hong Kong Buenos Aires

ISBN 0-439-32425-4

12 11 10 9   4 5 6 7/0

Printed in the U.S.A.   40

First Scholastic printing, February 2002

Designed by Kimi Weart
The text of this book is set in Nofret.

To my sweet Emily, with love,
and
special thanks to Lena V.

MAYA

LAST SATURDAY, I STUMBLED half asleep into the kitchen, aiming for a bowl of granola, thinking it was just any old Saturday morning. But when I came through the kitchen door, my little sister, Lena, yelled, "Maya's awake! Can I tell her? Can I, *please?*"

My dad nodded.

"Tell me what?" I asked sleepily.

"Daddy's taking us to Six Flags, Magic Mountain TO-DAY!" Lena screamed. "And we can each bring a friend!"

"Really?" I was suddenly wide awake. "Really?"

Dad's smile grew. "Eat something first," he said.

"YA-HOO!" I yelled. My sister was jumping around the kitchen and I jumped with her.

Lena was bringing Ann, of course. They always did

everything together. My parents called them "Salt and Pepper."

First I called Candace, because everyone in our group called Candace first for everything. That was just the way things were. But her line was busy, so I called Renée.

"Hi, Renée," I said. "It's Maya. Wanna go to Magic Mountain with me today? My dad'll take us!"

I'd expected Renée to squeal with joy or moan with disappointment, but there was silence. That wasn't really *so* strange, though, because Renée always thought and spoke slowly. I'd just thought that talking about a trip to an amusement park with tons of rides would speed her up.

Finally Renée said, "Gee, Maya, I um . . . I can't."

I knew her folks were going through a divorce and she was shuttling back and forth between their apartments, so I figured that was the reason she couldn't go. I could picture her serious face, her eyebrows knitted. Actually, Renée's eyebrows were so light, you could barely see them knit—you'd only see her forehead bunch up.

"Um, thanks," Renée added. "I'm, I'm really sorry."

"That's okay," I said, feeling sorrier for her than me.

I hung up and tried Candace's number again, but her line was still busy. I'd have waited for her to hang up, but the longer it took me to find a friend and get ready, the less time we'd have for the rides. It was a long drive to Magic Mountain.

So I called Brianna, but her mom picked up and said Bree wasn't home. I knew Brianna hated it when her mom called her Bree, but I didn't say anything. "She's on her way to Darcy's," Mrs. Cohen said. "Aren't you going too, dear?"

"To Darcy's?" I asked.

Brianna's mom just said, "Oh," and hurried off the phone. A gray, wispy sort of feeling started forming in my gut, where my excitement had just been. I took the phone to my room, shut the door, and punched out Candace's number for the third time. She answered.

"Candace?" I said, feeling suddenly a little shy. "It's Maya. I wondered if you'd like to go to Magic Mountain with me today."

"*Tooo-day?*" Candace said. The wisp in my gut grew to a gray cloud. "No, Maya," she said. "I won't be Magic Mountaineering *today*." Then Candace made a choking laugh and blurted, "Gotta go!" and hung up—bam. That "bam" felt like a door slamming in my face.

I didn't dare call Darcy. I bet they were all going there—without me. Well, maybe Darcy forgot to invite me. No, someone would have said, "Aren't you coming to Darcy's?" The gray cloud slithered up my chest. Higher, to my throat, choking me.

But couldn't it be a coincidence that everyone was

busy? Brianna's mom just thought I'd be going to Darcy's because we all hang around so much together, right? Wrong.

What had I done?

Had the girls been acting strange toward me? Did anyone act weird yesterday at school? I thought back. All I could remember was that Candace took one look at my new gray sweater with the loose lacy weave and said, "What corpse did you steal *that* from?"

I'd laughed. I'm not sensitive about stuff like clothes and Candace was right, it did look cobwebby! I knew that from then on I'd always see my new sweater as a shroud on a mummy. Candace had that effect on me. When I'd been so thrilled bringing a persimmon from my own tree to school, Candace had shuddered, saying the inside was the texture of snot. "Sweet red snot," she'd said. Instantly, that was *exactly* what it felt and tasted like. I'd gagged and spit it out.

I glanced at the mirror and caught myself chewing on my nails. None of the other girls bit their nails. Candace and Darcy collected nail polishes. Between them, they had every color under the sun.

How long had they been planning to leave me out of whatever it was they were doing today? The grayness curled around my head, squeezing.

Had anything happened in the lunchroom Friday? We'd all sat together as usual at our table by the window, and I couldn't remember anything odd. Unless it

4

was when I'd said we should start a baby-sitters club, like in the books. I'd thought it was a good idea and I knew we could make a ton of money in the neighborhood, but Candace and Darcy had stared at me as if I'd grown fangs. Then they looked at each other and burst out laughing.

I'd said, "What's so funny?" but they were laughing too hard to answer me. I'd looked at Renée. She shrugged. "What's so funny?" I asked again, but that made Candace and Darcy laugh even harder. Brianna smiled along with them. Then the bell rang.

On the way out of the cafeteria Renée said to me, "You know, um. Candace watches her brother and sisters a lot. Maybe she, maybe she thinks that's enough baby-sitting?"

Lena burst through my door.

"I told you to KNOCK!" I said.

"_Sorr-rry._ Daddy said we're leaving in fifteen minutes. Why are you _still_ in your nightgown?"

I imagined myself at Magic Mountain with Salt and Pepper shrieking in my ear on the rides, begging my dad for cotton candy and churros, giggling constantly. I liked them, but without a friend there for _me_ . . .

"I'm not going," I said.

"Huh?"

"Magic Mountain is stupid," I said. "It's for babies."

"Is not."

"Is too."

Lena ran from my room yelling, "Daddy, Maya doesn't wanna go!"

What was I going to tell him? It was a very big deal that my dad was willing to take us and spend that kind of money. We all knew that living in this neighborhood, renting this house, meant no extra money for stuff like day trips and treats. We hadn't been anywhere in ages. I couldn't stay home because Momma had just gotten a job as an interpreter at the hospital, and she'd be gone all day. Other girls were allowed to stay home alone, but not me.

My dad appeared at my door. "What's the matter?" he asked, already sounding annoyed.

"I just don't want to go," I said.

"Ten minutes ago you were thrilled," he said. "Weren't you the girl who jumped up and down cheering?"

I said, "Sorry."

"Did you get a better offer?"

"No."

My sister peeked around my door. "Well," Dad sighed. "Momma's gone to work and I'm taking Salt and Pepper. You want me to drop you at a friend's house or something?"

That's when tears filled my eyes. I suddenly had no friends. I tried to think of someone I could call. Someone from outside the group, some friend from before. But it had been so long, and I guess I'd dropped everyone else when Candace and her crowd had come along. Not dropped in a *mean* way, not with a BAM. I'd just sort of drifted away, faded out. If I called one of those girls now, I'd have to say *something* about why I hadn't called them in so long. Worse, they'd instantly know I'd been dumped. They'd hear the echo of Candace's "BAM!"

Maybe I should just show up at Darcy's, just walk in casual and cool and say, "Hey! What's up?" But I knew I couldn't do that. Most likely, I'd creep in all cowardly, cringing and speechless, like a dope. Worse, I'd whimper, blubber like a baby, beg.

"I'll be ready in a second," I said, not looking my dad in the eye. "I've just got to get dressed."

He nodded and left, closing my door behind him.

Renée

I KNOCKED ON THE bathroom door. "Mom?"

"Come on in," she said. I didn't want to come in. I wanted her to come out. She'd been in there all morning.

"Are you going to drive me to Darcy's?" I asked through the closed door. Actually, I must have said something like, "Are you um, um, going to um, drive me to um, Darcy's," because Mom said, "Try it without the ums please, Renée."

So I *carefully* repeated, "Are – you – going – to – drive – me – to – Darcy's – house?"

Satisfied this time, Mom answered, "Can't you walk?"

"I told you," I said. "I've gotta take my sleeping bag and stuff."

"Give me a second," she said. My heart sank when I heard her bathwater swoosh. It wouldn't be a second. She was still in the tub and hadn't even started her hair/makeup ritual. No ancient tribe took longer to prepare for their sacred ceremonies than Mom took to prepare for her day. My friends thought I was a slowpoke, but I was lightning compared with her.

Forty-five minutes later we were in the car. Mom was saying that my dad would pick me up from Darcy's tomorrow, then she'd get me from his apartment Sunday night. She wanted me to be ready to leave. She did not want to wait around his apartment for me. I already knew that.

"Darcy didn't invite Maya," I said, interrupting her.

"Well, Darcy is certainly free to invite whomsoever she pleases to her parties," my mom said.

"Everyone is invited but Maya."

"*Everyone*," Mom scoffed. "The entire seventh grade?"

"And Maya called me this morning to ask if I wanted to go to Magic Mountain with her."

"That was nice."

"Well, it made me feel . . ."

"Squirmy?" Mom said, finishing my sentence. I was going to say guilty, but squirmy was close enough, so I nodded.

"Life is squirmy, Renée. It's just one long squirm, birth to death." She wiggled behind the steering wheel and laughed. Then she said, "You're not responsible for someone else's guest list. Save your squirms for your own embarrassing mistakes."

"But I didn't know what to say when she—"

"Don't go borrowing squirms," Mom said. "That one's not yours. I suppose you could have boycotted the party, said, 'I ain't comin' unless Maya comes.' But what would that get you—besides uninvited to parties?"

"But—"

"But what?"

It didn't *feel* right, but I couldn't put it in words. When Darcy had called the night before to invite me to her sleep-over, and told me she wasn't inviting Maya, it gave me a stomachache. I'd hung up and called Brianna, but Brianna was like my mom—she didn't think it was my problem or hers either.

We pulled up to Darcy's driveway. "Have fun!" Mom said. "See you tomorrow night. Be ready!"

I got out of the car and lugged my stuff to Darcy's front porch. My mom honked as she drove off. I wished she wouldn't do that. The other mothers didn't *honk*.

Darcy's big sister, Keloryn, let me in. Whenever I wished I had a sister, it was always Keloryn I imagined. She was nothing like Darcy. Not that I didn't like Darcy, but Darcy had a sort of sneaky way about her. Well, not *sneaky* exactly, but kind of prickly. No, that's not the right word. Well, whatever Darcy was, Keloryn was the opposite.

She wasn't like other big sisters who always tried to embarrass everyone and act cooler than cool. "Hi, Renée!" she said, smiling her big, friendly smile. "Everyone's upstairs."

I dropped my sleeping bag and stuff on the pile and went upstairs. Darcy's staircase was wider than the stairs of my apartment building. I loved her stairs. I know it sounds silly, but I pictured myself dressed fancy, floating up those wide stairs, like in a scene from a romantic movie.

I followed the giggles to Darcy's room and opened the door. For a second I was confused, but then I realized everyone was wearing wigs! There was Darcy with long blond corkscrew curls boinging down her back instead of her own straight brown hair. Darcy is so small and thin that the big loopy curls looked like an octopus swallowing her headfirst.

Everyone was laughing and shoving to get to the mirror. "Better late than never!" Darcy said, seeing me at the door. She tossed me a black wig but I missed it. It looked like a shaggy dog at my feet. As I stooped to pick it up, I said, "My mom, she . . ."

"Let me guess," Candace said, stuffing her long dark hair into a strawberry blond wig. "Your mom went into slow motion, right?"

I smiled. "Right."

"It's worth it," Candace said. "She always looks like a million bucks." Then Candace looked in the mirror and said, "Yikes! *My* mom wore her hair like this as a teenager."

"You look like her," Brianna said.

Candace rolled her eyes. I knew she didn't like hearing that, because once when we were looking at old photos at her house, I'd said the same thing and she'd said, "But look at my mom now! She just let herself go full-bloat frump!"

I'd figured Mrs. Newman couldn't help getting older, and I still thought she was pretty, but I hadn't said anything.

Then Candace had showed me another picture of her parents, one taken before she was born. Mr. Newman had his arm around Mrs. Newman's teeny tiny waist, and they were both smiling their hearts out. They obviously adored each other. There were no photos in the world of my parents looking so in love, but I didn't mention that. Instead I'd said, "They look like movie stars. Look at your mom's waist!"

"Yeah, I wonder what my dad thinks of her waist now." Candace had squinted at me then and said, "What do you suppose made two good-looking people like that have so many kids?"

I'd shrugged. "That's what people do!"

"Yeah, well, your parents just had *you*. Even Brianna's

parents thought they got it right the first time, thought Brianna was enough. *Mine* had to go on after me, and have not one, not two," Candace ticked them off on her fingers, "but THREE more kids! I'm not going to throw *my* life away like that."

"Your mom seems happy to me," I'd said.

"That makes it even sadder," Candace said.

"It's sad that she's—that she's happy?" I'd asked.

"Her life is diapers and bottles and Nick's soccer games." Candace shivered. "What in the world has she got to be happy about?"

"I don't know about Brianna's parents," I'd said. "But my parents stopped at one kid because they . . . they didn't *like* each other!" Candace knew my parents were separated. But I'd never told her, or anyone, that the only reason they got married in the first place was because of me—because Mom was pregnant with me.

I put on the wig. It felt strange, tight. I wondered how women could stand that feeling. But looking down at the long black hair falling all the way to my lap, I figured it was worth the discomfort to suddenly be someone new.

Brianna pulled a red mass of curls over her own dark blond hair.

"There's a kid in our homeroom with hair that color," Candace said. "Darcy, what's that girl's name who sits next to me? Is it Nicole?"

Darcy shrugged.

"But she wears it in a fabulous, thick braid. Not a poodle-do," Candace said.

"Maybe I should wear this mop to the audition," Brianna said. "It's a comedy, after all."

"Audition?" Candace whipped her wigged head around.

"Yeah," Brianna said. "That group at the college that did that play last year? Tryouts are coming up again."

"Wow!" I said. "I hope you get a part. We all loved it last year."

"I suppose it's *possible* that lightning can strike the same place twice," Candace said. I wondered what she meant by that. I looked over at her. She was pulling on a platinum blond wig. That's my hair color! It was so weird seeing Candace in disguise, and weirder still to see her disguised as *me*! Her dark eyebrows and long black lashes looked strange with my nearly white hair. The whole thing was like a bizarre dream.

All the girls were themselves, but not—they looked so different in the wigs. Me too. I kept peeking in the mirror, wondering how my life would be if I really looked like that. I tossed my head, feeling the waves ripple down my back—longer, thicker, and even blacker than Candace's.

Darcy took off the blond corkscrew curls and was herself for a minute while she hunted through the wig pile. I didn't want to try on a different one. Mine felt perfect.

I watched Candace posing in front of the mirror like a fashion model, shoving her hips way forward the way they do in magazines. She put on a sulky pout, then a beauty queen grin, then that totally bored expression some models wear.

Suddenly she gasped and in a squeaky bimbo voice said, "I never should have eaten that grape yesterday! Now I'm completely obese!" She started fake weeping.

"I heard some models have their lower ribs removed," Brianna said, "so their waists will look smaller."

"I thought they just made themselves throw up all the time," Darcy said, pulling on a wig with short brown, wavy hair. She took one look in the mirror, then shrieked, "Hey, guys! Who do I look like?"

"MAYA!" Candace called out, dissolving into hoots of laughter. Darcy pulled the wig off as if it were on fire and flung it across the room.

Then Candace said, "Maya called me this morning," casual as can be.

"You're kidding!" Darcy gasped, eyes big and excited. "Did you *tell* her about my party?"

Candace nodded. "I did. I said, 'Well, Maya dear, honeycakes, sweetie pie, I'd just *love* to go to Magic Mountain with just about *anyone* else in the world besides YOU!' Then I told her we were all celebrating her absence here today."

Brianna's mouth fell open. Darcy snickered. You never know with Candace. Maybe she really did say that! But even if she didn't say that, she probably said *something*. I winced. Now Maya knew why I didn't go with her today.

I did not tell them that Maya had called me too. I let my long black hair fall across my face to hide my squirm. What else could I do? I wanted to ask why they suddenly hated Maya, but wouldn't that make me look stupid? Wouldn't that make me look like I was on Maya's side? Well, I thought, I *am* on her side. After all, she's my friend.

Candace put on the Maya wig and started nibbling on her fingers exactly the way Maya did. I felt like a traitor, watching her. She really did do a perfect imitation of Maya, even the expression on her face and her posture. I wondered how Candace would imitate me.

"Candace, *you* should come to the audition with me!" Brianna squealed. "You're an amazing actress, and we'd have a blast being in the play together."

"I think not," Candace said.

"Hard to picture Candace standing around on stage with no lines to say or anything," Darcy said. "No offense, Brianna."

Brianna smiled and looked at the floor.

Candace struck a pose and in a regal English accent said, "But of course, the chorus would simply never do. It's the starring role or nothing for me!" She smiled as if she were kidding, but I don't think she was.

Darcy

You'd NEVER KNOW IT if you saw her now, but years ago, my aunt was a model. After she quit, she gave all her old wigs to me and my sister, Keloryn. My mom suggested I bring out the wigs for my party, but I thought that was a lame idea. My mom is NOT an expert on parties. In fact, the only two parties my parents ever threw were their wedding, which was small and held in a judge's chambers, and a tea when my mom graduated from law school before I was born.

But it turned out my mom was right—my friends loved the wigs! Everyone was clowning around and having a blast. It looked like my party was a hit and I almost relaxed—but not quite. Every now and then I'd glance at the clock and my throat would close. We had so many hours left until tomorrow. What if Candace and everyone got bored? It would be my fault. My party means my fault.

Candace looked fabulous in every single wig. She was so gorgeous, and funny too. She could do impressions of people that were absolutely astounding. Her imitation of Maya was a scream!

Renée put on one wig and then just sat there in a trance. I didn't worry about it, though, because Renée gets quiet that way. Brianna says it's because of her parents' separation, but I think Renée has always been kind of moody. When everyone but Renée got bored with the wigs, we put on our suits and went for a swim. I don't know what Renée did. Maybe just sat up in my room wearing that witchy black wig and daydreaming. After a while she came outside and curled up in a deck chair.

Brianna floated around on the blue raft, knocking against the side of the pool and bouncing off to float in another direction, like a leaf.

I looked around at my friends and felt lucky. Sometimes, I secretly used our first initials to make up names for our group. It was lame, I know, but I liked to do it. Until yesterday, we'd had M for Maya, and my favorite names for us were Really Dumb But Cute Monsters, and My Big Dorky Rubber Chicken. Now it was time to drop the M, so I had to think of ones with just D for me, C for Candace, B for Brianna, and R for Renée. Dark Clouds Bring Rain?

Candace is a great swimmer and her dives are perfect, even when they're silly ones. She could probably be in the Olympics if she wanted to. She announced, "The Dive of the Shy," and timidly minced to the edge of the board, head down, shoulders hunched, then stepped meekly into the pool without making a splash. Next she did The Dive of the Oasis, crawling to the edge of the diving board gasping, "Water! Water!" and tumbling in. She hauled herself out, sleek as a seal, and wrung the water out of her long black hair, saying, "Any requests?"

"The Ballet Dive," Renée said, at the same time as I said, "The Bird Dive."

Candace bowed, saying, "Presenting the Ballet Bird." She flapped her arms and did a perfect pirouette off the board. I wanted to scream out to the whole world, "Eat your heart out, everyone! *I'm* her best friend! Me!"

When Candace was tired of swimming, we played cards. Candace suggested dress poker instead of strip poker. So over our swimsuits, we added layers of clothes. Brianna, who doesn't play games very well, was sweating to death in pants, socks, two shirts, and a hat.

Everything was going great, in fact, until about nine

o'clock. That's when my sister, Keloryn, came into the kitchen to ruin my life.

She looked around the table at us and asked, "Where's Maya?"

I turned to Candace. After all, it had been Candace who'd hated Maya first, and it was her idea not to invite her to my party. But Candace didn't say a word.

Renée spoke up, though. "Darcy didn't, um. Darcy didn't invite her," she said. Renée always acted gaga around my sister, like Keloryn was God.

"Why not?" Keloryn asked.

No one said anything, so I said, "Because I didn't _want_ to. Not that it's any of _your_ business."

Keloryn looked right smack at Candace and said, "I see." But Candace didn't give a hoot. She made a bored face back at my sister, as if Keloryn were dust.

If Keloryn got Candace mad, if Candace left or decided we were having a bad time, I'd kill my sister, I swear! Candace yawned and blinked like a cat. Keloryn headed out of the room. No one moved or spoke.

I had to prove where my loyalties lay. I had to show Candace and the others whose side I was on. I had to save my party. If Candace left, everyone would leave, or at least they'd want to.

I thought fast. The phone was lying on the counter right next to me. I could hear my parents laughing at some TV show, so I knew the coast was clear. I grabbed the phone. My heart thumped as I pressed the speaker button. I felt like I was on a climbing roller coaster as I dialed. The kitchen was electrified with a tingling charge—like that split second before the roller coaster plunges downhill, sucking the screams right out of you.

Maya

W E'D BROUGHT PIZZA HOME. Salt and Pepper were hyped up and giddy. Dad was beat. He'd had all the giggling he could stand. The two-hour drive to Magic Mountain had been hard, with Lena and Ann chattering in the backseat. I'd sat up front with my dad, trying to act like nothing was wrong.

I hadn't realized I was biting my nails until I tasted blood and saw that I'd gnawed my fingers raw. Dad probably noticed but he didn't say anything. He didn't even complain about my radio station. Somehow, his being so extra nice made me feel extra worse.

Waiting in line for the rides, I couldn't help picturing everyone at Darcy's house, having fun without me, talking about me. But once we'd taken our places on the first really fast ride, every thought was whipped right out of my head.

When Salt and Pepper were ready to puke and Dad said his brain was rattling loose in his skull, they stumbled off in search of snow cones. I got back in line and rode again and again, screaming myself hoarse. Roller coasters are great brain cleaners.

The drive home was depressing, though, knowing I was headed back to a world that was just as messed up as it was when I'd left the house that morning. I'd tried to tell myself it was all a mistake and there'd be a message on the machine when I got home, saying, "Where _are_ you, Maya? We're all waiting at Darcy's!" Or maybe I'd wake up and discover that this was just a really rotten dream.

But then I'd swing back to reality with a sickening, Tilt–A–Whirl spin and realize that no, this was not a nightmare, it was my life.

Anyway, we were just sitting down to pizza. Momma was telling us about her day. She worked in the emergency room mostly, but sometimes in other parts of the hospital, helping the new Russian immigrants explain their pains to the doctors and nurses, and translating what the doctors and nurses said back. My mother came here from Russia seventeen years ago and remembered how hard it all was in the beginning, so now she tried to make it easier for the newer newcomers. I was proud of the work she did and liked hearing her hospital stories, even though they were often really sad.

That day a woman had brought in her little boy, who'd crashed through a glass window and was all cut up. The woman was hysterical. When Momma tried to explain to her that no one would help her son until she'd filled out a bunch of paperwork, the woman went wild blaming my mother! But later, when the surgeon came to say the boy would be okay, Momma and the woman hugged.

Just as my mother told us that, the phone rang and I answered it, half expecting it to be that woman from the hospital. A muffled voice said something I couldn't make out, and I heard laughing in the background.

I said, "What?"

The voice said something else unclear. The words didn't matter; I suddenly knew who it was. Then Darcy's voice said, "I just wondered if your mother knew that here in America, dentists can put *white* caps on teeth instead of gold. You might want to mention that to her. And on the subject of dental hygiene, we were all wondering if you know what mouthwash is. It comes in bottles, usually it's green . . ."

I dropped the phone onto the cradle. Momma was looking at me. "It was just a crank call," I mumbled, trying my best to sound casual. "Just some kids."

The phone immediately rang again. None of us moved until it rang a second time. My sister, Lena, grabbed it and said, "Hello?" Then she said, "Okay, I'll tell her. Bye."

Lena turned to me and said, "Someone said to tell you it's not nice to hang up on people."

"Who was that?" my mom asked.

Lena shrugged. "She didn't say her name."

Ann tapped my arm. "It's true, you know. It *is* rude to hang up on people."

"What happened here?" my mom asked me. "Who was that calling?"

I wanted to say, "No one." Or, "Don't worry about it, Momma." Or, "It was a wrong number." But nothing came out of my mouth.

"This was someone you know?" Momma asked.

I couldn't answer. My mom grabbed the phone and dialed the number that reconnects you with the person who just called. I put my head down on the table and died, wondering if I had stinky breath for real.

"This is Mrs. Koptiev," Momma barked. "Who is this? . . . Who? . . . Well, a call came from you, a mean call." Then there was silence while she listened.

I looked up to watch her face. It was pale with anger. "Well, you tell your sister and those girls that next time, I call the police!"

"Keloryn Griffin, sister of Darcy," Momma said, hanging up. She peered at me. I didn't look at my dad.

"I don't get it," Lena said.

"Me neither," said Ann.

Mom reached for my hand. "These are horrible girls to hurt you." She shook her head in disbelief. "My Maya they chose for their cruelty?"

There was no stopping my tears then. They gushed out and I ran to my room. Behind me I heard Lena whine, "But I don't GET IT!" Dad told her to hush and eat her pizza.

Momma followed me. "They hate me," I told her.

"Hate," she spat. "Hate from such people means less than nothing."

"I don't even know what I DID!" I wailed.

"Did? You did nothing. This isn't about *did*. This is about bad girls being stupid. I would only love to go wring all their stupid necks!"

"How am I ever going to go back to school?" I cried, feeling like I was going to throw up.

"How? You just go. You ignore those girls and you're better without them. This isn't friends, this is dirt. This is less than dirt." Momma kept patting my back and trying to rock me. She didn't understand. Maybe things like this didn't happen in Russia.

Brianna

C ANDACE PUT HER sleeping bag right smack in front of the fireplace. I'd wanted to sleep next to her, but it wasn't meant to be. It was Darcy's party and she got there first, and Renée, who usually moved like a snail, beat me to Candace's other side. No big deal, no big deal.

I said, "I don't think boys have slumber parties."

"My bother's afraid to sleep out," Candace said. "But he's not normal." Candace always called her brother, her "bother." And her baby sisters "the twerps," instead of the twins. I thought she pretended not to like them so we wouldn't be totally jealous every second—she didn't want to sound smug about her perfect family, or for that matter, her perfect everything.

I asked, "Anyone met that new boy, Eric? He's in my art class. He's really, really cute." Candace looked interested. I wanted to call dibs on Eric, finders keepers, but that was dumb.

I pictured myself getting him to talk to me at school. Then the girls would waltz up and I'd have to introduce them. First he'd see how cute Darcy is, then how blond and feminine Renée is. But when he saw Candace, his eyes would pop out and he'd get that drooly look that boys get at the sight of her. By then he'd have totally forgotten the big-nosed girl he'd been talking to—me.

I sighed, but no one noticed. They were all staring into the flames. I heard Candace say, "Darcy, if you were an animal, you'd be a—let me think."

"You mean what animal she looks like or acts like?" I asked.

"Both," Candace said. "How about a whippet? You know, those pointy little dogs with rat tails and ribs showing?" Candace sucked her cheeks in. The firelight and shadows made her face look like a skull. "Skinny and fast!" she said.

Everyone laughed, especially Darcy. We always, always laughed, no matter what. I didn't know how everyone else felt about Candace's games, but I thought they were tests, like walking on hot coals or something, to prove how tough we were.

A few days before, we'd all been sprawled under a tree at the park when Candace told me that if I were a color, it would be blue. I hadn't been offended, praying that she'd meant a bright, interesting blue. But then a washed-out, blah-blue car drove by and Darcy said, "There goes Brianna!" and no one contradicted her. I probably just smiled.

That was colors. We'd done foods too, and I was a sandwich. Now it was animals. I knew they'd say something about my nose when it was time to do me. I hate, hate, hate my nose. I bet they were going to say I was an anteater.

"How about Renée?" Candace asked.

Well, if it was how Renée looked, it would have to be a white animal. She looked like a picture that had been mostly erased, or hadn't been colored in in the first place. She was like a glass sculpture of a girl. Everything about Renée was hard to see. Pale blue eyes; hair and lashes so blond, they were almost see-through. I thought of those clear, milky jellyfish, but just as I was about to say that, Darcy said, "A sloth."

No, I thought, that's not right. Renée was slow, but not stupid or lazy like sloths are supposed to be. You could die of old age before she got to the end of a sentence, but not because she was dumb. Renée was careful, watchful. "Not a sloth," I said. "A white owl. Minus the flying and mouse hunting," because Renée's a vegetarian.

Candace laughed. "A starving owl with a broken wing?"

"No, no, no!" I said. "An elephant, maybe?"

"She's not *that* fat!" Candace said.

"I don't mean *fat!*" I smiled apologetically at Renée.

"A tortoise," Candace decided. "And if Renée's a tortoise, who's the hare? You, Darcy?"

"I thought I was a whippet!" Darcy said.

I was next. I secretly prayed for strength and pretended to watch the fire while they decided about me, reminding myself that it was all about being a good sport.

Candace said I was some kind of a bird. The others agreed, probably because of my beak. "Not an eagle, though," Candace said.

"No, a sparrow!" Darcy offered.

I pictured myself pecking around, peck, peck, hop, hop, hop. A sparrow: plain, common, boring. But I laughed on cue when the others did.

"Sparrows are amazing," Renée said.

"Yeah, right," Darcy scoffed.

"No, really!" Renée said. "Remember when I had that ear infection? Well I, um, sat on the balcony watching this sparrow fly back and forth to her nest. Thirty-something trips in an hour! Her babies cheeped their heads off every time, as if they were, as if they were starving to death."

Candace said, "She should have pointed her beak south and kept on flying."

Renée stared into the firelight. "Well, I, um, I thought she was remarkable."

"Remarkably stupid, you mean," Candace said. Then she said, "Okay, guys, time to do me."

That was easy. We all instantly agreed that she was a large cat—a lioness or, because of her dark hair, a panther. Candace practically purred hearing that. Who wouldn't? A powerful, graceful panther sure beat a flappy gray sparrow, working herself to death fetching crumbs.

"Well, this cat is *hungry!*" Candace growled. "Beware, tiny creatures!" Darcy made a scared, whipped yelp and sprang to her feet. Candace chased her into the kitchen. Renée and I followed.

"What would Maya be?" Darcy asked, opening the pantry. "Some baby animal."

I was getting tired of the Maya thing, but Darcy was right—sometimes Maya was kind of babyish. "Puppy?" I said.

"A cockroach!" Candace laughed. "Quick! Step on it!" She jumped down off the stool to stomp an imaginary bug, grinding her heel into the floor.

Darcy yelled, "Gross!" and collapsed in a fit of giggles.

Then we were scooping ice cream, looking in Darcy's fridge, daring each other to try ketchup on vanilla, mayo on chocolate, when Darcy's big sister, Keloryn, came in.

"Mrs. Koptiev called," Keloryn said.

"Maya's *mother?*" Darcy shrieked. "What animal is *she?*"

"A bear!" Candace laughed. "From the Russian circus!"

I couldn't help laughing. It fit Mrs. Koptiev perfectly!

"What goes around comes around," Keloryn said, grabbing a plum and heading back out again.

"Your poor sister," Candace said—loud enough, I thought, for Keloryn to hear. "Who can blame her for being ticked? Another Saturday night at home alone!"

Darcy hooted as if that were the funniest thing in the world, but Renée's eyes got huge, staring at the door Keloryn had left through. Renée's got a thing about Keloryn. I don't, but still, sometimes Candace's gutsiness took my breath away.

candace

Darcy's whole house was tasteless, but the tackiest room of all was the den. And the tackiest thing about the den was the huge, showy fireplace. It just *screamed* "Look how rich we are!" But with the lights out, all I could see was the fire itself. It felt hot on my face.

It made my heart race just making small talk while two feet in front of us, flames reduced thick, hard logs to nothing but smoke and ash. I don't get why people think it's relaxing to watch fires. If they'd look closer and pay attention, they'd see that there is nothing leisurely about fire. It's *frantic*. The flames are starving! I almost said something about it to the girls lying around me, but what would be the point? They were jabbering away about teachers. They wouldn't get it at all.

It reminded me of last summer when my family went to Sequoia National Park. We'd been driving all day before we spotted our first sequoia tree through the car window. My dad pulled over to the side of the road, and everyone piled out to go take a closer look. I didn't really *want* to, because even from that distance the tree's size gave me the willies. So I stalled, helping my mom get the twerps out of their car seats while my dad and my bother ran ahead.

Eventually I made myself walk toward that gigantic tree as it got bigger and horrifyingly bigger. I always make myself do stuff that scares me, always. But by the time I was standing at the base of its mammoth trunk, I could barely breathe.

I looked around at my family. There was my dad, fiddling with his stupid camera. My bother was stalking imaginary bears with his toy gun. Even my mom was fussing with the twerps as if the tree towering over us was just any tree. Why did no one see what I saw, or feel as I did? Didn't they get it?

Then a woman park ranger in uniform came up and calmly told us that the giant sequoia was two or three thousand years old. Two or three *thousand*! And it had grown from a seed the size of an oatmeal flake.

She pointed to the black marks on its trunk and said they were from forest fires. Ancient and modern fires, many fires over the tree's long life, each burning a little deeper into its flesh.

That's when I got really dizzy. The black marks reached high up the trunk of the tree. Forty, fifty feet up. That meant the flames were way over our heads. There'd be no running from a fire that size. In a fire like that I'd be burnt to a cinder in an instant, as if I were nothing.

Everything about that forest was so many times bigger than anything in my imagination that suddenly, looming dinosaurs seemed possible. The whole scale of the world was off, shrinking me to the size of an ant. If that tree fell on me . . . if one of those fires kicked up . . . panic made my mouth go dry.

I wanted to go home, escape from that place where a speck of seed, a tiny spark, could grow so huge. Where things lived so much longer than I possibly could. The thought of my short life, compared with the life of the sequoia, gave me a hollow, aching fear. But no one else was upset. My dad told us to smile and he took a picture of all of us with the park ranger.

I couldn't eat or sleep that night. I thought I'd throw up just _thinking_ about those trees towering over our cabin, growing taller and taller. My mom thought I was weirded out from altitude sickness.

Now I looked at the baby fire in Darcy's fireplace, but I wasn't fooled. It was pretending to be tame and innocent, but I knew that given a chance, it could become a huge wildfire, raging higher than Darcy's house, devouring the whole neighborhood in an instant.

"The fire's so pretty," I heard Renée say. And Brianna sleepily agreed. I closed my eyes and dug deep into my sleeping bag.

Of course, if I'd *said* anything about the power or destructiveness of fire, the girls would all be quick to agree with me. They'd scurry to tell horrid fire stories, trying to outdo one another. They'd interrupt one another, falling over themselves to show how well they understood me—trying to prove that they felt just as I did. But left to their own meager imaginations, they all thought fire was pretty.

I pretended to sleep.

Maya

My room was haunted. Even in the dark I could see the rhinoceros I'd won at the carnival at Candace's church. I closed my eyes, but they popped back open.

My head ached from crying and from trying not to cry. My cheeks were chapped. I crawled out of bed, turned the light back on, and squinted against the glare.

I had to exorcise my room, purge it of ghosts, chant cleansing incantations, burn incense, light candles—do *something* to get those girls out of there. I needed to reclaim my room. Make it mine and only mine.

I started a pile on the floor: the rhino, the purple lanyard keychain that Darcy had made for me. Out of my drawer and straight onto the pile went the stack of Renée's homesick letters from summer camp. Next was

the autographed program from the play Brianna was
in last year. I didn't have to look at it to remember
what she'd written. "Maya, dahhhhhling, there's no
business like it! Forever, B!"

Candace, Darcy, Renée, and I had given Brianna a
bouquet of four roses, one from each of us. We'd gone
wild, applauding and cheering at the curtain call. Then
we'd run backstage screaming like rock fans, begging
for Brianna's autograph. I'd felt a little silly doing that.
After all, Brianna was only in the chorus, and she had
the smallest part in the whole play. She didn't even say
any actual lines. But Candace was never embarrassed
about making scenes, and she got us all going.

I sat down on the edge of my bed thinking there was
no saving my room—every inch was infested. I tried to
remember it before the girls. When I'd just moved here.

I'd loved this room from the first second. In my old
neighborhood some kids were rough. The big sister of
a kid in my class went to jail for shooting another girl
in the thigh with her dad's gun. We'd moved here right
after that.

Life was easier here and I hadn't been a bit homesick.
My folks were calmer and didn't watch me like hawks
anymore. They let me walk to school alone, which I'd
never been allowed to do in the old neighborhood. My
sister, Lena, met Ann right away and stopped following
me everywhere, which was great. The kids at school

were friendly and I'd made friends. Nothing tight like Salt and Pepper, but good enough.

Everything was nice, and then it got even better when Candace swooped down from the sky and scooped me up. My gut shrank, remembering how thrilled I'd been that day when she'd asked me if I wanted to "do lunch" with her. I thought I'd gone to heaven. She was popular and she'd picked me. Suddenly that made *me* popular too.

Renée, Darcy, and Brianna were part of the package. Once Candace had shone her light on me, they all took me in as their pal.

And now? Now that Candace had decided I was no longer worthy, did *any* of them give me another thought? I knew Darcy would do anything that Candace even hinted she wanted her to. But what about the others? Brianna wasn't the type to do anything drastic, like defend me on her own. But I couldn't believe that even Renée didn't care about me at least a little.

My eyes landed on my little cactus plant. We'd each bought one at the Earth Day fair. Candace had called them the Earth Sisters and said one day we'd all share a house and reunite the sisters in our big backyard. I threw the cactus into my trash can. It made a dull thunk sound in the otherwise silent house. It landed on its side and a clod of dirt tipped out. I shoved the can deep under my desk.

But I could almost hear the cactus say, "What did I do to deserve *this?*" I snatched out the trash can, stood the plant up on the bottom, poked the dirt back in, then slid it back under the desk. Maybe I'd give the cactus to Lena tomorrow, but I'd make her promise to keep it out of my sight.

Then there were the photo stickers of the five of us, making faces, cracking up as if life was just one big party. They were plastered everywhere, all over my school notebooks. *School.* The word made my insides wither.

I scraped and clawed at the two stickers I'd stuck on my light switch. It felt good, peeling off the girls' faces in little shreds, mine included. But the white stickum stayed stuck, a reminder of what had been there.

And what about the old-fashioned hand mirror Candace gave me for my birthday? Could I keep it? I wondered if I'd ever be able to look into it and not feel this gray cloud shrivel my guts.

I added the mirror to the pile, planning to put it all in Momma's box for the homeless in the morning. I hoped the things didn't carry their bad feelings with them. That's all some homeless person needs, I thought—a mirror that makes you hurt whenever you look into it.

RENÉE

We'd been talking about teachers from school, trying to imagine what kind of kids they'd been. Trying to imagine them our age, going to our school. It was funny picturing Mr. Adler, the principal, in regular clothes, acting like a boy. But then I noticed that Candace had stopped talking. She was just looking at the fire, not even listening to us.

I wondered if I'd said something to upset her, if any of us had. Then, without another word she burrowed into her sleeping bag and went to sleep. So maybe she wasn't mad or hurt or anything; maybe she was just sleepy. After that, conversation drifted off and soon everyone was asleep but me.

That always happened. I was always the last one awake at home too. When my dad still lived with us, I could never fall asleep until I heard his key in the front door. He was a jukebox man. Well, he had a lot of other kinds of vending machines besides jukeboxes, but that's what he called himself. He had jukeboxes and video games and pool tables in bars on the other side of town. When a machine broke or something, his answering service would call and out he'd go to fix it. No matter how late.

No one exactly *told* me that Dad's machines were in dangerous bars and bad neighborhoods, but I knew it. He hadn't taken me out on his route with him in years, but I still remembered the men slumped on bar stools, drunk in the middle of the day. I remember the way those bars smelled. I remember him taking the quarters out of a jukebox and dividing them up with the bartender. I also remember thinking that if he didn't have to support *me*, he wouldn't have to go to those places.

And on the nights when my dad wasn't on a service call, I'd still lie awake until he and my mom were asleep. I could always tell the second they were sleeping. Not just because their TV or their light went off or because they were finished fighting—but because there was a feeling, like the entire house had stopped holding its breath.

That's how it felt at Darcy's too. I knew her parents were sleeping. I knew her sister, Keloryn, was sleeping. All the girls around me were making little sleep noises like a basket of puppies. The fire in the fireplace was down to embers.

I wondered if Maya was sleeping. Maybe she was lying in bed staring at the ceiling. Maybe she was crying.

Darcy's sister probably thought I was as bad as the rest of them, and she was right. I knew what animal I was—I was a chicken. Otherwise, I would have *said* something. I would have stopped Darcy from calling Maya. Or I would have grabbed the phone and apologized to her.

After Darcy had made those calls, and we were going into the den to spread out our sleeping bags, Candace had whispered to me, "Sometimes Darcy's so *fierce*! Maybe we should enroll her in obedience school."

I wasn't sure what she'd meant. Fierce for making those mean calls? Obedience school, like a dog? So she'd obey her master better? Her master was Candace, right? I shivered. I hadn't said anything, but Candace must have seen my confusion, because as I put my sleeping bag next to hers she added, "There's really no reason to be *mean* to someone, just because you despise them."

I should have said something right then. If I hadn't been such a chicken I would have said, "But *you* were mean to Maya." Or had she been? Had Candace said bad things *to* Maya, or just *about* her? It was almost as if Candace were the queen, condemning Maya to death, and Darcy was the one who carried out the order. The executioner—an executioner who loved her work. And what did that make Brianna and me?

Was Brianna one of those people who in the old days went to executions to cheer and have a big party? And what about me? I watched Darcy make those phone calls too. Maybe I didn't cheer, but I didn't do anything to *stop* it either. And there was Maya, all alone, up on the gallows.

I remembered being at Maya's house a few weeks ago. I don't know where everyone else was. It was just Maya and me. Anyway, she wanted to climb the tree in her backyard. I always said no when she asked me if I wanted to, and I usually made up some excuse or another. This time, though, she asked me, "Renée, why don't you want to, really?"

"Promise you won't laugh?" I asked.

"Promise."

"Heights make me sick," I'd confessed. "Dizzy, pukey sick."

"Oh, we can cure that," Maya had said, as if it were no big deal.

"I don't want to cure it. I'm scared to."

Maya'd thought that was funny. "You're scared to not be scared?" She grabbed my hand and pulled me outside, saying, "If you climb up on the first branch, that really low one"—she pointed to it—"I'll get my mom to bake strudel."

I love Mrs. Koptiev's apple strudel.

Maya hauled me over to the tree. "Put your hands on the trunk," she said. "Feel how strong it is."

I felt silly.

"Go ahead, touch it," she said. "It's alive."

I made sure no one else could see me, then did as she said.

Maya didn't make fun of me, she never picked on me or laughed at me or bullied me, she just sort of coaxed me inch by inch, until I was sitting on that branch with both my feet off the ground! Maya beamed, proud as punch. But she wasn't satisfied.

Slowly, gently, she talked me into climbing up to the next branch. She told me to look around at the view. It made me woozy to look down, and my stomach lurched, so I can't say that I *liked* it up there, but it wasn't really so horrible either.

Then Maya talked me back down. I'd been very glad to get my feet back on the ground, but still—I'd done it! We'd done it! Maya and I sat under the tree, feeling good, feeling close. I know it probably sounds dumb, but it was a big deal to me, and it seemed like a big deal to Maya.

That Monday she brought a whole plate of her mom's amazing strudel to the cafeteria at lunch. And she didn't tell the other girls why.

And a few days later, when we were all together and

Candace said we should tell what our worst fears were, Maya didn't say anything about my problem with heights. I was just about to tell the girls about it myself and get it over with, but then Candace said, "Me first. I'm terrified that my mom is going to get pregnant again and have more babies." She'd said it seriously, but I knew that it was just a jokey fear, so I didn't really have to confess mine.

I looked up at Darcy's den ceiling and swore to myself that I'd call Maya tomorrow as soon as I got to my dad's. I would. I'd call her and say I was sorry. And who cares what Candace and everyone thought of that? I didn't have any reason to hate Maya, and I wasn't at all sure why everyone else did.

And what did it matter what the other girls thought of her? It only mattered what I thought, right? I rolled over and tried to fall asleep, but I couldn't get comfortable.

What if Maya had done something really awful, though, I thought, looking around at the sleeping girls. Candace's hair was spread across her pillow like a giant dark spider. Darcy was so tiny that her body barely made a bump in the blankets. Brianna was curled in a ball.

What if Maya had done something really mean to one of them? Something mean that I just didn't know about? Then it would be weird to call her and act all friendly. She must have done something pretty bad, because Candace really seemed to despise her. And Darcy had *loved* making those phone calls.

Maybe I wouldn't call from my dad's. Maybe I'd wait till I got home to my mom's tomorrow night and send Maya an E-mail. That way I wouldn't actually have to hear her voice. But what would I write? A piece of wood broke and fell in sparks in the fireplace, making me jump.

There was a stone hearth around Darcy's fireplace, then carpeting. We had all hardwood floors. My mom was very persnickety about her floors. When she wanted to rearrange the furniture, she made me help her lift everything. Breaking our backs beat scratching her floors. I thought wood floors were mean. Well, not *mean* exactly, but sort of cold and unfriendly. My dad's apartment had carpeting, but it was stringy and got caught on my toes when I was barefoot.

I wiggled my finger into Darcy's soft carpeting. It was deep, up to my second knuckle. I was going to have carpet like that one day. When I grew up, I was going to have lots of carpeting and maybe colorful rugs on top of the carpets. And no stiff furniture—I'd have all big stuffed, soft things, lots of cushions. My whole house was going to be like one giant pillow.

The girls would come over to my pretty house and they'd look around and say, "Oh! So this is the real Renée!"

But would Maya be there too? I decided that if I

didn't call or E-mail her tomorrow, I'd at least for sure act totally normal with her at school on Monday.

But how would *she* act? I shuddered, imagining myself having to walk into school with everyone hating me. I wouldn't be able to do it. If I were her, I'd run away.

Darcy

I WANTED CANDACE TO STAY after everyone else so we could talk about my party, but her mom came early to take her to Sunday school. Once Candace was gone, I wished everyone else would leave. I planned to get out my journal, write about my party, and maybe list all the names I could think of for our group, dropping Maya's M. But Renée and Brianna and I went back up to my room.

"What do you want to do?" I asked them.

Brianna shrugged. "What do you want to do?"

Renée picked up that same scraggly hag wig and petted it like it was a black cat. I knew she wanted to put it on again, but it wasn't the same without Candace.

"You could grow your hair out," I said, "long like that. Dye it black." Renée was so ghostly pale, with such wispy white feathers for hair, and she'd looked so lame in that black wig, that I was really only kidding. But Renée nodded as if she were seriously considering it.

"Do you think you'll um, dye your hair and stuff?" she asked me and Brianna.

"Sure," I said. "But my mom won't even let me wear makeup till I'm sixteen. My sister didn't mind, but I do."

"Keloryn didn't want to wear makeup?" Renée asked.

"Keloryn is weird," I reminded her.

Brianna said, "I got a rash from the makeup I had to wear in that play last year, remember? It itched something awful. I practically scratched my face off."

"All makeup isn't like that," I said. "That was probably cheap or something." Then I turned to Renée and said, "I bet your mom would let you wear makeup right now if you asked her. She'd probably let you borrow hers." I sighed.

"My mom, um . . . she wants to um, get plastic surgery," Renée said, frantically twirling the black hair around her finger and wrinkling her nose in disgust.

"Plastic surgery—that's like when you have your fat cut off and your boobs made bigger, right?"

Renée nodded.

"Is your mom going to get breast implants?" Brianna asked, her big brown eyes getting bigger and rounder.

"No." Renée shivered. "She has these, these folds over her eyelids that she hates."

"*Eeeeww!*" I gasped. "She'd let them slice her EYE-BALLS?"

Renée nodded. "And she um, she wants a bigger chin."

I looked at Renée and we both burst out laughing. Brianna didn't. She just sat there looking stiff as a plank.

I said, "Well, I'd like a nose right smack in the middle of my forehead! And, Doctor, could you please make me a second mouth, here off to the side, so I could talk with my other mouth full?"

Renée laughed. But Brianna sounded mad when she said, "Why should people have to keep something ugly on their faces just because they were born with it? That's not fair."

"But there's nothing so um, so ugly, really, about my mom's chin," Renée said.

"I didn't mean that," Brianna said.

"And to get CUT! Sewn!" I said. "Ish!" Then I told them about how my aunt, the ex-model, had her ears pinned back. Only one of them worked. So until she had it done over, she looked entirely lame, like a dog cocking one ear at a noise.

Renée laughed, but Brianna just sat even stiffer. Then Keloryn called upstairs, "Brianna, your mom's here!"

We trooped downstairs and stood around the front hall while my sister talked Brianna's mom's ear off. Keloryn worshiped Brianna's mom because she taught at the university and had a Ph.D. Maybe Keloryn thought Mrs. Cohen, or should I say *Doctor* Cohen, could get her a recommendation or something. My sister was *very* college-bound, good grades, honor society, that stuff.

Eventually Keloryn let Brianna and her mom leave, and Renée and I went into the kitchen. "What was bugging Brianna?" I asked.

"I think maybe, um. I'm not sure but I wonder if she um . . ."

"Spit it out, Renée!" I said.

"Well, we all know she um, you know. She doesn't like her nose."

"You're right!" I said. "Brianna's probably dying for a nose job. Especially if she's planning on being an actress."

"Oh, I don't think she really, *really* um, wants to be an actress, do you? And anyway, actresses can have all kinds of noses."

"Well, actresses can," I said, "but not stars. Movie stars have to have perfect little noses, like Candace's." We were quiet awhile, thinking about that. "It would be funny, you know," I said, "if Brianna really did become a star, famous and stuff. It would make more sense if it were Candace."

Renée nodded, then said, "Can I ask you a question?"

"Sure!" I said.

Then out of the blue, Renée said, "What did Maya, um, what did she do exactly?"

I took a gulp of air and felt myself get hot. I should have been ready for this, but I wasn't and I felt entirely trapped. I had no idea why Candace had turned against Maya so suddenly. No idea at all. But I couldn't admit that to Renée.

She was waiting for my answer.

I said, "You don't *know?*" as if that were shocking. Then I added, "It's really kind of personal, with Candace, and if she doesn't want you to know, well . . . I'd like to tell you, really I would, Renée. But it's just not my place to blab. Sorry."

Renée nodded, as if that made perfect sense.

Brianna

SHE'S A NICE KID, Darcy's sister," Mom said in the car.

"Keloryn?" I said. "She's okay. Kinda spooky though."

"Spooky?"

"Well, she's so *good!*"

My mom laughed. Then she asked me how the party was, and how late we stayed up.

"I dunno. Late," I said.

Mom sighed. "Does that mean you're going to be out of sorts all day?"

"I'm not sure."

"Remember, you promised to do your homework the second you got home," she said.

"I remember, I remember." Then I said, "Mom? How do you feel about plastic surgery?"

"Funny you should ask that. There was an article in the *Times* just this morning about the proliferation of clinics performing cosmetic surgery without adequate medical backup."

"Huh?" I said.

"Storefront clinics, where surgeons are qualified but they're not in or near hospitals. So if something goes wrong—if the patient starts hemorrhaging, that means bleeding uncontrollably, or goes into cardiac arrest, which means the heart stops functioning properly— they aren't equipped to deal with it. The patient has to be transported to a proper medical facility, losing valu- able time."

"Yuck!" I said.

"Imagine dying for a face-lift!" Mom said. "That takes vanity to new heights!"

I thought about that for a minute. If God created us to look the way He wanted us to look, then maybe He got mad when we messed with it. But if *that* were true, I thought, then why would He let people invent plastic surgery?

"But what about in a hospital?" I asked my mom. "Where they have everything right there in case of an emergency?"

"Any operation is dangerous. The anesthetic alone is always a risk."

"Renée's mom wants a bigger chin," I said.

Mom turned and looked at me, eyes wide. "A bigger *chin*?" I nodded and smiled a little. It did sound kind of funny.

"To have surgery to save your life is one thing, but elective surgery . . . well, doesn't that sound foolhardy to you?"

I shrugged, wondering how old you have to be to get an operation without your parents' consent. And I bet it cost a fortune.

Darcy

Renée's dad didn't come until around eleven. By then I was all talked out and tired. Renée's dad was weird. He wiped his feet on the mat for about twenty minutes before stepping into our front hall. No wonder Renée's mother was divorcing him. Renée's mom wasn't so bad. She was really young, and she had shelves and shelves of makeup and perfume and stuff in her bathroom. My mom's cosmetics were a bottle of dandruff shampoo and a lipstick.

And Renée's mom dressed great. Not flashy like my aunt, the ex-model, who thought she was still a teenager. Renée's mom didn't wear short skirts or tight, low-cut tops. She just always looked nice. I bet she'd get a new husband in no time.

My mom's closet held a dozen dark suits in a row, all almost exactly the same. Under that stood low–heeled, nearly identical pumps, black, mostly. Mom's wackiest fashion statement was when she wore a pink blouse instead of a white one.

After Renée left, my mom came into my room, dressed in her lawyer clothes. That meant she was going to the office, even though it was Sunday. She put her fists on her hips and said, "Keloryn told me something very disturbing last night. I didn't want to confront you in front of your friends, but we need to talk about this right now."

I knew she meant the phone calls. "Keloryn's a jerk," I said, busily neatening my bookshelf.

"That's not the point," she said. "The point is that I did not raise my daughter to be a bully. I need you to explain your actions toward Maya."

"We made a phone call, so what?" I told her. "It was just a joke."

"A joke?" Mom said. "I need to hear more than that."

My mother and her needs! She *needs* me to clean my room. She *needs* to know about that phone call. She *needs* to work on Sunday. I didn't say anything.

"Darcy," she said in her stiff lawyer voice. "You and your pals did not invent cruelty and exclusion. It's been going on since Eve. But it is the work of small minds. I need to know that you're bigger than that. That you're going to make amends to Maya. That you have a conscience, and regret victimizing that poor child."

"I don't like Maya."

"That, Darcy, is irrelevant. The point is, you acted un- kindly toward another human being, and you need to think long and hard about that."

I felt a guilty cramp in my gut, but I was absolutely NOT going to let my mother see that. And maybe the phone calls were a little mean, but at least now Maya knew she was history, and she wouldn't have to find out in person. At least she'd know to stay away from us at school. So actually, I sort of did her a favor!

I couldn't tell my mother that it was Candace who'd brought Maya into our group, and Candace who de- cided to butt her out. That this was between them and had nothing to do with me. Did my mother actually expect me to be friends with someone Candace hated? *Ish!* That would be so complicated, sneaking around, trying to see both of them. Maya wasn't worth it.

I'd never thought Maya was anything special in the first place. In the beginning, Candace thought Maya was cool because she'd known girls who'd shot each other, and she'd lived where there were gangs and she couldn't go outside after dark. Whatever.

"Look at me when I'm speaking to you," my mother said, her voice getting shrill.

I turned and looked her right in the eye, using all my strength to keep my face completely blank. I knew she hated that. We stared at each other awhile and then she said, "You leave me no alternative but to ground you. You're to come straight home from school, alone, until you apologize to both Maya *and* Mrs. Koptiev. Understood?"

I said nothing. That was so unfair! Further proof that my mother had no clue about my life, zero sympathy and subzero understanding of what girls like me have to deal with. She'd never for a second been best friends with someone like Candace.

My mother was always saying how pleased she was that I had a lot of friends and stuff, but she *also* said she didn't think I was a good judge of character. Once she said she didn't know what I saw in Candace!

Didn't she realize that the whole reason I was popular was because of Candace? How could she be proud of me for being Candace's friend and at the same time hate Candace? She just didn't want me to be happy. I bet she's jealous that I was having fun and that I was more popular than she or her beloved Keloryn ever were or could ever hope to be! I knew they'd both be thrilled if I was just another lonely nerd like them. Well, tough.

"IS THAT UNDERSTOOD?" my mother's voice was louder, her face redder. "Answer me!"

I didn't.

"And, as humiliated as I am by your conduct, I will swallow *my* shame and call Mrs. Koptiev myself to apologize. And, of course, I'll make sure you've made your apologies. Needless to say, I do _not_ appreciate being put in this position, Darcy."

My mother was looking right at me, but I knew she couldn't see me. She'd never been able to see me for who I was. When my mother looked at me, I could tell she just saw a blur of disappointment, a blur of all the things she wanted me to be that I wasn't.

She left my room and I crumbled. Now I was grounded—all because of my creepy tattletale sister. I hated her. I reached for the phone to call Candace and tell her what had happened. I wanted to tell her what a witch my mom was. The witch and the snitch—that's _my_ family. But then I remembered that Candace was at Sunday school.

I looked across my room at the box of wigs and remembered Candace clowning around, making everyone laugh. As mad as I was at my mom and my sister, I still felt lucky. The witch and the snitch and the whole rest of the world could try all they wanted to destroy me, but I'd always be fine—I had Candace!

candace

My MOM PICKED ME UP alone! The twerps' car seats were empty. Not even my bother was along for the ride.

I tossed my stuff into the trunk and said, "My bag's packed! This is our chance!"

Mom smiled at me, puzzled.

"Our chance to make a break for it!" I explained. "By the time Daddy figures out how to get the twins dressed, you and I could be halfway to Paris!"

Mom laughed. "Well, maybe we have time to stop for a doughnut, at least."

"On our way to Paris?"

"On our way to Sunday school."

"Come on, Mom, we could change our names, wear sunglasses. They'd never find us!"

"What's the matter, love?" Mom asked. "Did something bad happen at Darcy's?"

I sighed. "No. Nothing *bad* happened. Nothing good happened either. It was just . . ." I suddenly felt tired. "It was just plain ol' plain."

How could I explain that sometimes Darcy, Brianna, and Renée felt like leeches? A swarm of parasites, living off my flesh. My mom would say that I should be flattered, she'd say I was lucky to be so important to my friends. My mom lived for other people; she *liked* being needed. At least that's how she acted.

"What did you do? Watch a movie?" Mom asked.

I shrugged. I didn't have to ask what *she* did while I was gone. That was no mystery—she ran after the twerps and folded laundry. I shuddered. What a life! I wondered if Mom ever secretly dreamed about escape. I bet at least once in a while, in her heart of hearts, she wished she could rewind her life, erase the tape, and do it all over differently.

"Nick has a soccer game this afternoon," she said. "Do you have any plans?"

Oh no, not again. I braced myself and muttered, "No, I don't have plans." I knew what was coming.

"Then would you mind watching Tess and Beth?"

I moaned.

Mom pretended to ask, but she didn't really ask. If I answered, Yes, I'd *mind* watching the twerps, she'd sigh that sigh of hers and make me feel like a selfish pig. I don't know why her sigh made me feel so guilty. The twerps weren't *my* responsibility. I certainly never asked her to have them.

No fair! No fair! I chanted in my mind. If I'd said it out loud, my mom would have said what she always said: "Who said life was fair?"

Mom couldn't afford baby-sitters to watch the twerps because she didn't have a job. And she didn't have a job because she was home watching the twerps! Round and round it went. It was crazy, a craziness that left *me* baby-sitting for free all the time, like it or not.

"Joanne has the flu, so I told her I'd pick up Jake and take him to the game for her." Mom looked at me sheepishly. She knew I thought she did way too many favors for her friends. I didn't see the other mothers offering to drive *my* bother to games when my mom was sick. And NO ONE offered to watch the twerps, EVER, except me—not that I actually offered either.

Then Mom said, "I'd take the twins with me, but you know they're all over the place. Last week I missed Nicky's one and only goal because I was busy chasing Tess out from under the bleachers."

I looked over at her. She'd missed a spot brushing her hair. It was smooth all around except that one snaggly hank in back. And she was wearing a sweat suit again. It made her look like a cow.

Oh no! Was she pregnant? I felt a hot panic burn

through me. Not more babies! I whipped my head around and stared through the windshield, fighting tears.

No! She wouldn't do that to me—not *again*. It's just those ghastly sweats, I told myself.

"So, do you want to stop for doughnuts?" Mom asked.

I found my voice and managed to say, "Doughnuts are fattening."

"Well, there aren't any celery stands open this early," Mom said. "So what do you think?"

I took a deep breath, telling myself that I was just in a foul mood because I'd stayed up so late. "Mom," I said, "why don't you shoot those sweats and put them out of their misery?"

She laughed as if I were joking. "I'll just duck down and drop you," she said, smiling. "I'll circle the block and no one at the doughnut shop will know you even *have* a mother. How's that?"

I rolled my eyes at her and she laughed harder.

I thought of Renée's picture-perfect mother. Hair, makeup, nails, clothes. My mom could be much, much prettier than Renée's mom, if she'd only spruce herself up a bit. But Mom dragged herself out of bed in the morning and pulled on the same sweat suit she'd worn the day before.

Whenever I said anything about the bagged-out

knees or the baby-food stains, she just laughed and said something like, "Well, I guess my career as a cover girl is over!" As if caring about her looks would be ridiculous.

But I'd seen pictures of her before she had me, and she was really beautiful. She could have been a cover girl if she'd wanted to. But no, she decided to have babies. *Lots* of babies. I just didn't get it.

Brianna got it, though. The way she coochie-cooed the twerps, I bet she was going to have tons of kids. I could just see her calling on *me* to help the way Mom's friend Joanne was always calling on her. "Candace! I have a cold. Could you drive my kids all over town, then stop and pick up some groceries and fix us lunch?"

I felt my skin get hot. I had no intention of ending up like my mother, Caretaker of the Universe—taking care of everyone but herself. I'd say, "No, Brianna. You breed 'em, you feed 'em!" I laughed out loud and my mom smiled over at me.

"Nick's game will probably go until about two-thirty," she said. "But I expect Daddy home by one. So, really, you'll only be on duty about an hour or so. Okay?"

"Whatever," I said.

"Thanks," Mom said, patting my leg.

I wanted to say, "Mom! You could have done *anything* with your life! You were so cute! You even got good grades!" But instead I said, "You have a big knot in your hair in the back."

My mom reached up and raked at it with her fingers. I wondered if she was going to go to my bother's soccer game like that. Probably.

Maya

My LITTLE SISTER, LENA, knew something was wrong and was dying to know what had happened. But my folks kept shushing her and sending her out to play with Ann. I could see that Momma was aching for me, and that made me feel even worse. She made waffles, my favorite, but I couldn't eat.

I climbed as high as I could in the persimmon tree out back and wished I could just keep climbing forever, let the world shrink away to nothing beneath me—my house, my school, my ex-friends becoming nothing more than an anthill underfoot. Or that I could just spread my wings and soar away.

My foot slipped and I had a split-second sensation of falling. I caught myself and froze, hugging the trunk of the tree until my heart calmed down.

Then I realized that if I'd fallen, everyone would think I'd jumped. If I'd died from the fall, they'd think it was suicide. The girls would be sure I'd killed myself over *them*! I could imagine how important that would make them feel—that they could hurt me so badly that I'd think my life wasn't worth living. They'd mourn and act sad, but deep inside they'd feel great that they were so powerful.

I climbed down very, very carefully, branch by branch.

Brianna

CANDACE CALLED ME when she got home from Sunday school. She said her mom had taken her bother to his soccer game, leaving Candace on duty with the twerps. She asked if I'd come over and help, seeing as I was their honorary auntie.

I said I'd love to. I loved the twins and I loved, loved, loved Candace's topsy-turvy, noisy house. Candace once said that my house reminded her of an old library. "Not just because of all the books," she'd said. "It's the dusty old drapes and the whole dark silence." I'd been hurt, but she was right. Candace always spoke her mind, and she usually said what the rest of us thought but were too timid to say. I admired that about her.

My house *was* like an old library. Not a bustling busy one, though; mine was just quiet. My mom taught microbiology at the university. Dad taught astronomy. They didn't *believe* in TV—as if TV were a religion.

And when I was a baby, when other kids were reciting nursery rhymes, my parents trained me to rattle off the genus and species of all the plants in our yard. When other kids were wishing on stars, I was learning the constellations. And when I started losing baby teeth, there was no visit from the tooth fairy. Instead, my parents had our dentist demonstrate tooth growth on a model of the human jaw.

I knocked on my mom's office door and told her I was going to Candace's. She turned to squint at me over her reading glasses. I thought of the animal game we'd played at Darcy's last night. Mom would be a mole—underground, long-nosed, nearly blind. My dad would be a tall, skinny, silent animal, something even ganglier than a giraffe. An insect? A walkingstick or praying mantis, maybe.

I loved them, of course, and wouldn't really, really want them to be *totally* different. But I didn't want to be like them when I grew up.

My parents' idea of fun was to lug the telescope and microscope out to the godforsaken desert—poke in the dirt all day, peer at the stars at night. It was as if they were at work twenty-four hours a day. My mom said that proved they were in the right careers, getting paid to do what they'd do for free anyway.

But isn't it possible to be a scientist by day, then play

slide trombone in a Dixie band or drums in a rock band at night? Watch TV? Be in plays? Have parties with noisy friends on the weekends?

"Did you do your homework, Bree?" Mom asked. I wished she'd stop calling me that baby name, but it was pointless to say so. She hadn't heard me the last nine million times.

When I'd told Candace that I hated being called Bree, she'd wrinkled her perfect nose in sympathy and said, "I don't blame you a bit. Isn't Brie a smelly kind of sticky cheese?"

Candace didn't like being called Candy. But when she said, "Candy rots your teeth," and flashed her perfect pearly whites, people listened. I'd never, ever heard *anyone* call her Candy twice.

"Oh, by the way," Mom said, "Maya called yesterday after you left for Darcy's."

I said a quick prayer that she wouldn't ask me about Maya, and it worked. Mom turned back to her computer and said, "If you're absolutely positive that all your schoolwork is complete, you may go, but be home by dinner."

I walked the long way to Candace's, so I wouldn't have to pass Maya's house. But when I got to the big stand of shaggy banana trees near the monastery, I remembered her begging me to play in there with her. Maya had wanted to pretend we were apes, or Tarzan or something. I'd thought that was so dorky. And what if someone saw us? I'd die.

It wasn't that I didn't like Maya; it's just that she got so *happy* about stuff. Not that happy is bad. It's . . . well, this sounds really snobby, but Maya was like a little kid. She wanted to climb trees, ride bikes around without going anywhere—just play.

Sometimes it was okay, but other times, being with Maya was like wearing shoes I'd outgrown. I looked away from the banana trees and shook thoughts of Maya out of my head. I wondered instead what I should wear to school Monday that might catch Eric, the new boy's, eye.

Renée

MY DAD ALWAYS WANTED to do something special on our Sundays together, but I didn't much want something special. I just wanted to go home and curl up in a ball. But he looked worried and asked me if I was feeling all right, so I said, "I'm just tired. We stayed up really late at the sleep–over."

"Had a late night myself," Dad said.

For a split second I wondered if he could have had a date. But then he continued, "Apparently there was an all–out cowboy brawl at Nickless Betty's."

I remembered that it used to be called Nick and Betty's Lounge, but then Nick died and my dad jokingly told my mom and me that it was Nickless Betty's now. I'd thought that was funny but my mom got annoyed. "That's exactly the kind of insensitivity I mean!"

she'd said and huffed out of the room. I hated memories like that, memories that started out fun but ended in a cringe.

"Got the call about eleven," Dad was saying. "I got there, and nine cue sticks were broken in half, and some joker had slashed the felt off the pool table. The boys were all in a lather because the jukebox was dead. But no one thought it might be because _they'd_ knocked it over." My dad laughed and shook his head. "Cowboys," he said.

I didn't know what to say. I was glad my dad thought I was old enough to hear about his work, but I hated to picture him walking into a bar full of angry drunks late at night, all alone.

"Want to go to a movie, maybe?" I asked.

"Absolutely!" he said. "As long as it's not about cowboys."

The only movie that was at the right time and close by was one I'd seen last week with my mom. I didn't say so, though, because I was afraid it would make him feel bad. I really didn't mind seeing it twice. And it wasn't my dad's fault that he wanted our Sundays to be special. It was his only chance, I guess, to be _Dad_.

I wished he could relax, though. In the old days, between service calls and his daily jukebox route, he used to just pick up the newspaper and disappear behind it. I missed that. I missed everyone acting normal. I wished I could just _be_.

After the film was over, we picked up Thai food because my dad knew it was my favorite. Actually, I was tired of Thai food, but there we go again, everyone trying to guess what will make the other one happy and no one guessing right. Maybe after the divorce was over and done with, we could all just go back to being ourselves. In the meantime, Dad and I went back to his apartment so I could eat my 900th dish of pad Thai and chicken satay with spicy peanut sauce.

I looked at Dad's telephone, and Maya's number ran through my mind, ruining my appetite. But I didn't call. I was ashamed of being such a wimp, but I didn't know what to say to her. And wasn't life hard enough without having to worry about Maya?

I reminded myself that I really didn't have anything to feel guilty about. Mom was right, it wasn't *my* squirm. It wasn't *me* who didn't invite Maya to Darcy's party, and it wasn't me who made those nasty calls or said that stuff about her breath or her mom's teeth. I fought down a wave of guilt, telling myself that as long as I acted nice tomorrow at school, I had nothing to feel bad about.

My dad had fallen asleep in his chair. His mouth was open; he looked dead. Well, not *dead* exactly, but old. It made me sad to picture him here, alone all the time. No one to listen for his key in the lock. No one to know if he got home safely from late-night service calls.

I knew he was going to be embarrassed that he'd

conked out while I was visiting. I rustled my homework papers, then thumped my book, and saw him
lurch awake out of the corner of my eye.

I looked at the clock. It was too late to call Maya
tonight. I felt like a creep, remembering last summer.
That's when my dad moved out and I was sent to that
horrible sleep-away camp. I'd been so lonely, I thought
I'd die. It was Maya who'd written me cheer-up letters
every single day. None of the other girls did that.

Then a car horn honked. I'm sure the whole apartment building heard it. My dad sprang to his feet.

Oops, my homework was spread all over the table. I
gathered it up as fast as I could, remembering that I'd
meant to help Dad with the dishes. I promised myself
that next Sunday I'd be more helpful and better com-
pany too. Well, there aren't many dishes from take-out
Thai anyway, right?

My dad walked over to the window and looked
down at Mom's car. He didn't wave or anything. I
kissed him, told him I'd had fun, and dashed out the
door.

When I got to the car, my mom said, "I specifically
asked you to be ready!" instead of hello.

Brianna

Tess, ONE OF THE TWINS, shot out Candace's door and ran naked into the front yard just as I got there. When I nabbed her, she squealed with delight. I carried her inside and Candace rolled her eyes. From the way she said "You're such a natural with babies," I couldn't tell if she meant it as a compliment or an insult.

After I wrestled Tess into a diaper and trapped both twins in high chairs, Candace said, "What did you say the new boy's name was? Because we got a new kid in my Sunday school today."

My heart went thump. "Eric."

"No, this guy was Jeremy. He just moved here. He's nice."

"I don't know if Eric's nice or not. Haven't talked to

him yet," I said. "He sat way across the room in art." Then I remembered and said, "*Maya's* in my art class. That'll be so weird tomorrow!"

Candace smiled at me.

"We sit next to each other," I explained. "What am I supposed to say to her?"

Candace shrugged, as if that were *my* problem.

"Well, what should I *say*? How should I *act*?" I asked, hearing myself whine.

Candace blinked at me as if she barely recognized what species of creature I was. I tried to read her face, but there was nothing else written there.

Beth dropped her sippy cup and started to howl. After we got her calmed down, Candace laughed. "Wouldn't you love to have seen Maya's face when Darcy called her last night?"

No, I would *not* have loved to see Maya's face, I thought. I'm sure she was freaked. Probably cried. Ick and double ick! Why would I want to see that? And I was now completely dreading art class.

"But Candace," I said. "How do you *want* me to act with Maya?"

"Me?" Candace asked incredulously. "You're asking me how I want *you* to act?"

I nodded, feeling like a total fool, an ant, a nothing.

"And should I tell you how to walk?" Candace asked. "Talk? Think? Be? My God, Brianna, I'm not your mother!"

"Well, I can't *hate* Maya, I mean, I can't *hate* hate her, like she's the worst person that ever lived," I stammered, sounding like Renée. My heart beat faster. Why did it feel daring not to hate someone? I got confused, could feel myself blush.

"You *like* Maya?" Candace asked, her voice full of scorn.

"No, not particularly," I said, not sure anymore what I thought about *anyone*. "It's just that I'm sick of the whole Maya thing. It's boring."

"Oh, really?" Candace asked. "Well, Brianna, I'm so sorry to have BORED you!" She picked up a magazine and started leafing through the pages as if she were alone in the room. I watched the twins rub applesauce in their hair.

I could barely whisper when I said, "I don't even know, really, why everyone's so mad at her."

"We're not *mad* at your little friend." Candace sneered, flipping her magazine onto a chair. "We just think she's *boring*. Mind if I take a shower?"

She didn't wait for my answer, just walked out of the room. I wiped the twins' faces and let them down from their high chairs. Candace's shower ran for a long, long time. My parents always made me take short showers to conserve water.

Candace's dad came home after a while. He seemed surprised to find me watching his babies. The twins ran to climb his legs as if he were a tree. He asked where Candace was. I didn't hear the shower anymore.

"In her room?" I suggested. Mr. Newman raised his eyebrows the same way Candace did. A few minutes later I got up and walked home—to my quiet, quiet house.

Darcy

I CALLED CANDACE LATER and said, "I'm grounded!" But I never did tell her why I was grounded, because she didn't ask. She wanted to talk about my party. Actually, she only wanted to talk about Brianna.

"Don't you think Brianna acted like a turd?" she asked.

I thought quickly back over the party, trying to re-member what lame thing Brianna had done.

"Well, she called Renée an *elephant*," Candace said. "If I was Renée, I would have decked her."

"Do you think Brianna meant it like that?" I asked.

"Don't *you*?" Candace asked, as if I were entirely stupid or kidding or something. It made a chill go up my spine. Candace continued, "And who is she to call Renée an elephant? Brianna's the one with a trunk!"

I was about to tell her that Renée thought Brianna wanted a nose job, but I didn't have a chance because Candace was saying, "No, she's a cow! A big old, sway-backed moo cow. Those eyes of hers!"

I laughed. Brianna did have cow eyes.

Candace went on, "Don't you just see her in a little flowered apron, fussing over all her grubby little cow-ettes?" Candace put on a slow, dumb voice and said, "Ho–hum, having babies, chewing my cud."

I giggled.

"I tell you, Darcy, sometimes I think the world is turning me into my mother! Forcing me to spend my life taking care of everyone but myself! I mean, it's not Brianna's *fault* or anything, and maybe she doesn't *mean* to, but sometimes I feel like I have to remind her to breathe! I practically have to wipe her butt like she's one of the twerps!"

I had a creepy moment wondering if Candace in-cluded me in "everyone she had to take care of." But then she said, "Brianna actually asked *me* what *she* should say to Maya tomorrow! Can you believe that? She asked me how I *wanted* her to act!"

I pretended to be shocked. "Brianna asked that?"

"Oh, so Brianna can audition for that play all by her-self," Candace continued. "But somehow she can't make any other decision without me. What does she do when I'm not there? Just sit like a lump with her hands in her lap?"

I said something or other. Candace sounded really upset, and I knew it was best to just let her roll.

"Brianna's parents must be horrified!" Candace continued. "Here they are, science professors, and their own daughter has no more curiosity about the world than a cow!"

I certainly didn't remind Candace that Brianna got all A's.

"Oh, excuse me, I forgot about her fabulous acting career," Candace said sarcastically. "What a coincidence that she gets parts in the university plays, where she just happens to have not one, but *two* parents on the faculty. I wonder how many strings her parents will pull to get her a part this year."

I laughed.

"I dread sitting through another one of those shows, don't you?" Candace did not wait for my answer. She went on, "And let's say she *does* become an actress: How does she plan to raise all those baby cows of hers? Does she expect *me* to come and baby-sit? Does she think that *that's* what I'd want to do after all these eons of watching my bother and the twerps? No, she probably thinks she'll be so rich and successful that she can hire a full-time, live-in staff! Nannies, maybe a butler, gardener, cooks, maids, chauffeur, hair stylist . . ."

Candace paused to catch her breath and I added, "No doubt Brianna will have at least one dog groomer, a few stable boys, a pastry chef."

"Tennis coach," Candace said, finally laughing. "Personal trainer, masseuse?"

Candace and I laughed until my mother made me hang up.

I'd been right all along. I'd never thought Brianna would last. Back when Candace first took up with her, I hadn't said a word, just added a B. If Candace would bring in some girls with names starting with vowels, I could come up with actual WORDS! But now, drop the B for Brianna. That left C, D, R, Cows Don't Rate.

I knew the reason Candace brought new girls into the group was because she was so friendly and curious about people. She thought *everyone* was fascinating, for a while at least. She got excited about them and then she was finished. I just waited it out—no threat to me. I knew I'd always be Candace's best friend, and that's what mattered. That's really *all* that mattered.

Apparently my sister had been eavesdropping on my telephone conversation, because when I passed through the kitchen she said, "Brianna's next, huh? It should be your turn in no time." I kept walking and didn't even look at her.

"I'm looking forward to it!" Keloryn called after me.

Maya

"MAYBE YOU'LL NEVER laugh about this," my dad said as he left for work early Monday morning, "but one day it won't hurt quite so badly." That was his only mention of the whole thing all weekend.

I wanted to stay home from school more than I'd ever wanted anything in my life. But Momma had threatened to call all the girls and their mothers and tell them what she thought of them. I'd talked her out of it, but I knew that if I skipped school, that's exactly what she'd do.

I was trapped. I stared at the clothes in my closet. Opened every drawer. I wanted to wear something that no one could possibly think anything about. Camouflage. Something that made me invisible.

Clothes were crucial to Candace. Her outfits were

worked out to the last detail. And she always noticed what everyone else was wearing, down to the shoes. Darcy and Brianna did too.

But even though they'd advised me constantly, I could never quite pull it together. Candace would toss her long black mane and say, "Nice try, kiddo," making me feel like a little girl playing dress-up in Mommy's old clothes. She hadn't said it *meanly*, though.

Candace had a way of saying what she thought without seeming to judge. Sometimes I believed it was because she was so tolerant and wise. Other times I suspected it was because she didn't care. Me and the other girls thought about Candace constantly, trying to keep her happy. But I suspected that Candace never really thought about us. We were just there, like the air.

And if it wasn't Darcy, Brianna, Renée, and me buzzing around her, I bet it would just be some other girls. And maybe Candace wouldn't even notice the change. It was almost as if Candace was a force of nature, oblivious to her own effect.

But maybe I was totally wrong. Maybe she felt horribly guilty about dumping me. Or else, maybe when she said that stuff about my clothes, about my mom's accent, things like that, maybe she'd *meant* to sting me. Maybe it was a test, to see how much I'd take before I'd fight back or leave.

But it wasn't just *me* Candace said hurtful things to. She did it to all the girls. She liked playing those riddle games that left us gasping for air. And we all took it with a smile. Why did Candace think that was fun? And why did the rest of us always go along with it?

But when Candace had said stuff about the way I dressed, I'd really believed she was trying to help, and that she thought it was kind of cute of me not to be all clothes conscious. "Fashion–Free Maya!" she'd called me once, giving my arm a friendly squeeze. Remembering that squeeze made my eyes sting.

Today of all days, I wished I'd paid attention to her fashion advice. I'd love to walk into school, just this once, in a drop–dead fabulous outfit.

But then I remembered the way Renée dressed. She didn't even *try* and Candace never said a word about it! Renée's mom was a fashion plate and wanted nothing more than to dress her up like a paper doll, but Renée just stuck to her guns and wore jeans and T–shirts every day of her life.

I yanked a T–shirt out of my drawer. I'd dress like Renée. That was as close to invisible as I could get.

Renée

BEFORE I'D DECIDED exactly what to say to Maya, I got
to the corner of Maple, where we usually met on our
way to school, and I saw her. She was about half a
block away, coming toward me. My first instinct was
to duck behind a tree, but that was stupid. My second
impulse was to keep walking as if I hadn't seen her,
and that's what I did for a few steps, but then that felt
stupid too.

I knelt down and pretended to tie my shoe. Then I
glanced over my shoulder to see how fast she was
coming and she was completely gone—as if she'd gone
up in smoke!

Maybe I'd only imagined her. Maybe Maya was hiding—from me? It was weird to think of anyone being
scared of me. I hurried on to school, telling myself that

I really didn't have to worry about her until lunch hour, because she wasn't in any of my morning classes. By then I'd know exactly what to do and say.

Darcy and Candace were by the gate at school. When I got to them, Candace said, "I really want to apologize for Brianna, for what she said to you."

"To me?" I asked.

"I couldn't get it out of my head all day yesterday," Candace said.

"Get what out of your head?"

"You don't have to act brave. I know it hurt your feelings."

I had no idea what Candace was talking about, but Darcy must have known, because she was nodding sympathetically.

I looked from one to the other.

"Shhhh!" Darcy said. "Here she comes!"

I turned around and saw Brianna walking up, waving. I was the only one who waved back.

"She said you looked like an elephant!" Darcy whispered to me, her breath hot on my ear. "Remember?"

I laughed. "Oh, come on!" I said. "She didn't, she never, I mean, well, Brianna didn't mean anything!"

"Honestly, Renée," Candace said, exasperated. "Do I even have to tell you when to be *mad*? What am I"— she looked from me to Darcy, then back at me—"a life raft? Here's Darcy, kicking and thrashing around in the water, practically pulling me under." Darcy laughed as

Candace flailed her arms, imitating a panicked swimmer. "And here's Renée." Candace went limp. "Dead weight, hanging around my neck, saying, 'Should I swim? Should I um, um, um, be mad?'" I laughed a little and probably blushed. Then Candace said, "And here's me, just trying to swim to shore!" She smiled her big friendly smile as if to say "No offense." Or "Just kidding."

Brianna came up to us and said, "Hi."

"We think you owe someone an apology, Brianna," Darcy said in an icy tone.

"Me?" Brianna said. "I owe someone an apology?"

"You know *exactly* what you did," Candace said. "Don't play dumb."

"Maybe she's not *playing* dumb," Darcy added. "Maybe she really *is* dumb!"

"This is silly!" I said, recovering a bit from Candace's comments. "Brianna didn't hurt my feelings."

Candace turned to me with an expression of pity. "You're so sweet, Renée," she said. "Too sweet. And we aren't going to let anyone treat you like that."

"What are you talking about?" Brianna asked, her voice shaky. "Tell me!"

I think my mouth just hung open. I know Brianna's did. Over Brianna's shoulder I saw Maya walk way, way around us, shooting glances at us as if we were going to charge her like a pack of wolves. Then the bell rang. Darcy and Candace headed for the north door.

Candace looked back over her shoulder and said, "Think about it, Brianna," then walked away.

Brianna's eyes were darting around. I could hear her breathing. I tried to figure out what to say, but sometimes my mouth and brain don't seem to work together. Finally I said, "Whatever it's *really* about, it's NOT about you saying, well, that I was an elephant."

Brianna said, "Huh?" Then, "I think it's because I told Candace I didn't hate Maya."

"I don't hate Maya either," I confessed. "I don't hate anyone."

"Me neither," Brianna said, looking worried, like that was the wrong answer. We walked in to school and split up to go to our classes.

My first class was P.E., and I was way out in the outfield all alone with my thoughts. My parents were falling apart, my friends were falling apart. I could picture myself falling apart limb by limb, scattered arms and legs, vertebrae and ribs—like a mess of fried-chicken bones after a meal.

I looked around at the other girls on my team and wondered if any of them had ever felt that way. They all looked so happy: Rhonda pitching, doing jokey windups; Gloria on first base doing a cancan; Allison, shortstop, paying no attention at all, bending over to examine something. A flower? A ladybug? Then there was me, in the outfield, picturing myself as a heap of gore and dismembered bits.

candace

I'D BEEN SITTING right next to Nicole all year, but I'd never before noticed that her hair was like fire, flickering gold and red. She always wore it trapped tight in a thick braid as if it were a dangerous secret weapon that she had to keep strict control over.

I could picture one little strand working itself loose and lashing out like a spark. It would melt the rubber band that held the braid and suddenly all the hair would burst free! Let loose, it would take on a life of its own, whipping through the classroom, devouring everything in sight. Whoosh! The entire school reduced to ash.

I leaned over and said something to Nicole about her hair, and she blushed as if I'd guessed her secret power. No, that's silly. Of course her hair was only hair—amazingly fabulous hair, but just hair nonethe-less. And she'd blushed just because she'd blushed.

But still, there had to be something different about someone who grew such extraordinary hair, didn't there? Could hair like that grow out of an average head?

I tried to talk to Nicole, but Darcy kept buzzing around me like a mosquito.

"Wanna do lunch?" I asked Nicole in a whisper, and she laughed back, "Sure."

Darcy

IN HOMEROOM I WATCHED Candace lean over to the girl sitting on the other side of her and say, "I'm so jealous of your hair! I'd do anything to have hair like yours. Every day I just sit here and count the colors in it."

I was pretty sure the girl's name was Nicole, and it was true, she did have pretty hair. Red. In a thick braid. Nicole looked dazzled by Candace's sudden attention and flattery. She blushed, smiled shyly, and said, "But Candace, *your* hair is so fantastic!"

Candace smiled back at Nicole and said, "Let's trade!"

I admit I felt a tiny twinge of jealousy as Candace whispered something to Nicole that I couldn't hear. Here we go again, I thought, Candace and her girl collection! Now I'd have to hear about Nicole, hang around with Nicole—replace Brianna and Maya with

Nicole. I wondered if Renée already knew her. Now our initials would be C, Candace, D, me, R, Renée, N, Nicole. Cat Dog Rabbit Newt? Still no vowel! I smiled to myself but then looked over and wondered what I'd missed. Candace and Nicole were laughing about something.

I knew just how Nicole felt. I could remember how I'd felt when Candace first discovered me—like I'd been huddled in the dark and Candace brought the sun. It happened when Ms. Goodman put us together to do a science project in third grade. At first I'd been afraid that Candace would be disappointed to get stuck with me as her partner, but she wasn't. In fact, she'd seemed thrilled, as if she'd always wanted to know me. The very first day she'd asked me if I wanted to "do lunch," which meant sit with her in the cafeteria. From then on everyone knew I was Candace's best friend and they were all jealous, whether they admitted it or not.

Then her mom had the twins and Candace made me an honorary auntie. Without thinking I'd blurted out that I wasn't too crazy about kids. The second I'd said it, I regretted it. That sounded so ungrateful! What if I'd hurt her feelings?

But she wasn't mad. She'd squeezed my arm and said, "That's what I love about you, Darcy. I can't stand babies either! They look like boiled shrimp and all they do is cry."

That's when Candace and I started making up stories about the twins. Sometimes we said Beth was the evil incarnation of a psycho we called Bad McFoe. We called Tess, the other twin, T.T., short for Terrible Tess, McFoe's partner in crime. Other times we said the twins were not really earthlings at all, but were sent down from planet Zorp to destroy Candace with their evil poop bombs and acid spit-up.

Candace would call me and whisper, "I heard McFoe and T.T. plotting to murder me in my sleep! They've got my bother in on it too! Can I sleep over at your house tonight?" Or she'd ask to copy my math homework, saying the Zorps had used her paper in one of their shifty communications with their home planet.

It was our secret. Everyone else was wild about the twins. Brianna, especially, thought they were the cutest things on Earth. I remember when Candace made *her* an honorary auntie. Brianna was thrilled. She didn't see Candace wink at me behind her back. And a lot of good the honor did Brianna! Candace was entirely disgusted with her now. Well, that *was* a pretty mean thing Brianna said about Renée.

Sometimes I wondered what would have happened if Ms. Goodman hadn't put me and Candace together. The thought made me shiver. But I told myself that we would have probably found each other one way or another, eventually.

I wondered if Candace even remembered that science project. It had been entirely lame. It was about hatching chickens, but none of our eggs hatched. We'd made our parents buy little stuffed Easter chicks the night before the project was due, and we glued them all over the poster board. Ms. Goodman said we were hopeless. It was a blast being hopeless with Candace. Before that, I'd taken school so seriously, like my sister, Keloryn.

Back then Candace had been best friends with that girl—what was her name, Risa? Yeah, Risa. And Risa had been so jealous of me, she'd looked positively green! Candace had hated that. She thought jealousy was tacky. I wondered what had become of Risa. She was in my class last year, wasn't she?

I bent over my desk and smiled at Nicole around Candace. She should know that she'd been picked by me too.

Maya

I KNEW IT WOULD BE torture, and it was. First I saw Renée walking to school and I had to hide. My family had moved from one end of Los Angeles to the other, doubling our rent, to get away from fear, and now here I was in safe suburbia, taking cover and watching my back. I ducked between two cars and crouched there, peeking out till the coast was clear. But what was the point? I couldn't hide every second of the day. They'd get me eventually. Get me and do what? I knew they weren't going to pull knives on me, but still, I was ter-rified.

When I got to school, I saw the girls bunched to-gether exactly where we met every morning. Luckily, they didn't see me. I sneaked the long way around them and slipped inside the building and into my homeroom. I no longer thought of them as individual girls. Now they were one big, ugly danger.

I got all the way to my first class and safely to my seat before I let myself breathe freely. While Ms. Kaye was scribbling on the board, I looked around the classroom wondering who knew. They'd know soon if they didn't already. They'd all know I'd been thrown out of the group, and everyone would wonder why. They'd all think I had done something bad. They'd be afraid to talk to me, to be seen with me.

How was I going to get through this day? I caught myself gnawing at my cuticles and shoved my hands into my pockets.

Then the bell rang and my heart started to hammer again. Here goes round two, I thought. Should I rush out, race to my next class, try to beat the crowds? Or wait until the halls were empty and make my break then? I decided to stall.

If I made it to my second class, I'd be safe. But my stomach lurched when I realized that after that came art, and Brianna was in my art class! We sat right next to each other.

Everyone from my class had left, and the room was filling with the next load of kids. Time to go. I took a deep breath and darted out the door. Head down, moving fast.

I made it past the library. Almost there! I quickened my pace, turned the corner—and there they were, dead ahead: Candace, Darcy, and a girl I didn't know with red hair. There was nowhere to hide, no crowd to get lost in. Why had I waited until the halls were empty? That was so stupid!

I heard Darcy's voice, like a knife through my skull. "Well, look who's here! It's Maya! Nicole, do you know Maya?"

I tried to scoot past but Darcy blocked me. "Something *wrong*, Maya?" she mocked.

I didn't answer, just kept my eyes down. All I could see were the girls' feet. I was sure they could hear my heart thumping. Darcy moved in closer, shoving her face right up to mine. I could feel her breath.

"Maya," she said, "I asked you a question. Candace, didn't you hear me ask Maya if something was wrong?"

DO NOT CRY! DO NOT CRY! I told myself.

Then Candace said, "I gotta get to class." Her feet moved away with the other girl's. I heard her say, "What do you have next, Nicole?" Candace's voice was normal and calm, as if nothing in particular had just happened—was happening.

"Social studies," the girl said.

Darcy leaned even closer to me and whispered, "See you later, Maya. I promise." Then she hurried after Candace.

I stood paralyzed for a second before I looked up. I was shaking all over and felt like I was going to pee on myself. But at least I hadn't cried. I glanced behind me in time to see Candace, Darcy, and the other girl turn the corner. Gone—for now.

Brianna

I WENT TO MY FIRST CLASS and sat down, but I couldn't pay attention. My skin felt crawly. I had to order myself to blink. Eyes felt jammed open, open, open. Was this how Maya felt? Was this God's punishment for my not sticking up for her? For being glad it was *her* and not *me*? Maybe God had been testing my loyalty as a friend, my worth as a person—and I'd failed!

Had it mattered to me at all that Maya must have been totally freaked out by Darcy's phone calls? Truth-fully—no. Until Candace had turned against *me*, I'd felt nothing about Maya being dumped, except that it wasn't any of my business. Why had I thought that? Of course it was my business. I was supposed to be her friend! I could feel myself turning hot with shame. I hated people like me!

When Darcy called Friday to invite me to her sleep–
over and told me that she wasn't inviting Maya, I'd just
said, "Oh," sticking my head in the sand like an ostrich,
pretending the world wasn't out there. And later, when
Renée called to talk about it, I'd just pushed my stupid
head deeper underground. Now it was payback time.

I told Mr. Van Witter I had a headache, and he sent
me to Nurse Edith. Walking to the health office I could
practically feel the waves of gossip rippling from class–
room to classroom. Me and Maya, the talk of the school.
Both heaved out on the same weekend. Not together.
Each alone.

Nurse Edith took my temperature and told me to lie
down on the cot. She was going to call my parents but
they both taught classes till noon. Then she pulled out
my emergency card. I remembered that the name on it
was Mrs. Newman, Candace's mom. Everyone had her
on their cards because she didn't have a job, unless
you call four kids a job.

"NO! Don't call Mrs. Newman!" I begged. "I feel bet–
ter already. See?" I jumped up off the cot.

"How miraculous!" Nurse Edith said. "If only all ill–
nesses were so easily cured."

I looked at the floor tiles.

"Well, Brianna, then I guess you can return to class,"
she said.

I glanced at the clock. Almost time for second period.
Second period language arts meant waltzing into Can–

dace's clutches. I sat back down on the cot and told myself to blink.

Nurse Edith reached over to pat my hand. "Why don't you just tell me about it, dear," she said. She was round and sweet faced, like Cinderella's fairy god-mother. Her voice was kind. Next thing I knew, I was streaming tears. I told her the whole story. She never looked shocked, even when I told her what an ostrich I'd been about snubbing Maya.

Nurse Edith asked me what I thought I should do. I didn't know.

"What do you think your parents would suggest?"

My parents? They wouldn't get it, I thought. They'd think it was stupid. They had no idea that there was more to school than schoolwork. I shook my head. "This isn't their thing," I said.

Nurse Edith nodded as if she understood that too. "Well, Brianna, what do you think is the right thing to do?"

I thought a moment. "Be nice to Maya?" I asked.

"That sounds like a good place to start," she said. Then she asked me if I was ready to return to class.

"No."

She got up and walked across the room. "I have paperwork to do," she said. Then she sat down at her desk without seeming to give me another thought. I watched her work. I watched the clock. A kid came in with a bloody gash in his arm from woodworking class, and Nurse Edith just snapped on gloves and cleaned it up without looking grossed out.

Second period ended, third period art began. Maya was in art. I bet she was totally, totally, totally relieved that I wasn't in class. Eric wouldn't notice. I watched the clock some more. The hands moved very, very slowly.

Maya wasn't hiding her head in the sand in Nurse Edith's office, I realized. She was out facing it. I could never, never do that—go through my day as if everything were okay, knowing Candace and Darcy were talking about me, hating me.

I moaned, remembering secrets I'd told them. Cringe. I'd told Darcy about kissing Dan O'Neill at Candace's Halloween party. I'd been sure that meant he was going to be my boyfriend. But that Monday morning at school he walked right by me without even saying hi, as if he didn't know who I was.

I'd freaked out, was a total, total, total humiliated mess. I'd pulled Darcy into the bathroom and told her everything. She was really sweet and swore she'd take my secret to the grave, but I bet she was blabbing the whole story right this second. By the end of the day Dan and everyone else in the whole school would be laughing at me. Oh no, I thought with a fresh wave of horror, I'd even told them I thought the new boy Eric was cute!

Right before lunch Nurse Edith looked up and said, "So, what do you think, Brianna?"

What did I think? I thought I was going to die, that's what. Candace and Darcy were out there, waiting to tear me to shreds. Maya would be there seething with hate for me too. Maybe she'd revert to the ways of her old neighborhood and shoot me!

"I think I should stay here a little longer," I said.

Nurse Edith smiled at me. I could tell she did not agree. I gathered my stuff slowly, Renée-style, and thought about leaving school. I could sneak out the back door, hide in the bushes, somehow get out of here. And go where? And explain it to my parents how? And even if I got away with it today, what about tomorrow? I was doomed.

Nurse Edith patted my head on my way out. My feet weren't working right. I was sure my nose was bright red from crying. That always made it look about ten times bigger than it already was. I prayed I wouldn't run into that new boy Eric—or anyone else.

ReNée

I ADMIT, I DIDN'T RUSH to the cafeteria. I took maybe a little longer than necessary to put my stuff in my back-pack. Then I walked the long way to my locker. I didn't absolutely have to stop at my locker, but I kind of had to.

As slowly as I was moving, though, I guess Maya was moving even slower, because she showed up at the cafeteria after me. I got out of the lunch line and went back to where she was. When she saw me coming, her shoulders hunched and she stared straight ahead. The expression "scared stiff" came to my mind.

The thought that Maya was that scared of me was very embarrassing, but as I walked toward her I real-ized it was sort of thrilling too. I'd never had so much power before. I could go over there and make her happy, or I could go over there and make her ab-solutely miserable.

I said, "Hi, Maya," and gave her what I hoped was an apologetic smile.

"Hi," Maya said, nervously peeking at me sideways, her face still stiff.

I knew I was supposed to say something else, but what? The line moved up and I moved up with Maya.

"Hey! No cuts!" a boy behind us yelled.

I didn't respond. Neither I nor Maya said anything at all. Then someone tapped my shoulder. I looked around and Brianna was there. I was so glad to see her that it took me a second to notice that she looked aw-ful, like she'd been crying.

"Hey! What's going on here?" the boy behind us complained again.

Maya didn't seem relieved to have me and Brianna there. She looked braced, trapped, like a deer sur-rounded by snarling wolves. She expected us to start nipping at her, I think.

"We, we come in peace," I said, and smiled a bigger smile at Maya. She must have been holding her breath, because it came out in one big whoosh, and we all laughed a little.

Darcy

NICOLE SAT WITH US at the lunch table under the window where Candace and I always sat. They traded sandwiches, both curling their lips at my tuna. Then Candace asked Nicole if she wanted to come to the mall with us after school and Nicole said, "Sure." I knew that if she had any other plans, she'd break them.

Then I remembered I was grounded. It had slipped my mind entirely. "Hey, Candace," I said, "I can't go to the mall today. I'm grounded, remember?"

Candace looked blank.

"Forever grounded," I said. "Until I apologize to Maya *and* her mother. My mom is such a witch!"

I expected Candace to be sympathetic. To be horri-fied for me, or at least disappointed. But she just peered closer at me and said, "You plan to *apologize*?" as if that would be criminal, as if the very idea were entirely repulsive. Well, the idea *was* repulsive. I didn't have to mean it, though. I just had to do it, right?

Candace nodded toward the lunch line and said, "Now's your chance, Darcy."

I looked over and saw Maya, Brianna, and Renée going through the line. Why was Renée with *them?* We weren't mad at Renée. And after the awful elephant thing Brianna had said about her—well, Renée just had no pride. It made perfect sense that Maya and Brianna would stick together, cry on each other's shoulders, start a rejects' club, but how entirely weird that Renée would contaminate herself like that.

I knew there was no way Candace would take Renée back now that she'd gone over to *them*. Candace would be like a mother bird, flicking its baby out of the nest after a human touched it and got human stink on it. I shook my head at Renée's stupidity.

Fine, I thought, let Renée starve like an abandoned chick. She's made her choice! At least I won't have to listen to her ummming anymore. But it did feel a little weird to be down to just C, Candace, D, Darcy, and now N, Nicole. Chicks Don't Need?

"Well?" Candace said, raising her eyebrows and interrupting my thoughts.

I looked at her, then at Nicole, then back at the girls in line. I was about to say that I'd dubbed Renée, Brianna, and Maya The Rejects' Club, but suddenly everything felt wrong. Candace's eyes were blank, and I could almost have sworn that Nicole was smirking.

Forget it, I thought. I'm not going to go apologize to anybody! I'm gonna sit right here. But then I can't go to the mall after school, and that means Candace and Nicole will go themselves—without me. It was only one little trip to the mall, but I felt—no, I *knew*—that I had to be there.

Couldn't I just tell my mother that I'd apologized to Maya? No, she was planning to call and check. Well, maybe I could do it later this afternoon, when no one was watching.

"Go on, Darcy," Candace said. Then she waved her hand and said, "It doesn't matter. I'm tired of the whole thing, Brianna and them. It's all so boring."

So maybe she didn't really care. Maybe she wouldn't actually mind if I just did this apology real quick. Then I could go to the mall with her. I'd just go and apologize to Maya and it wouldn't be a big deal. I didn't have to be friends with her or anything. I just had to say, "I'm sorry." Just say the words, then come right back. No big stink. I got up.

Brianna

On stiff legs, like Frankenstein's monster, I clumped toward the cafeteria, but I couldn't go in. I knew this was my punishment. I deserved it but I couldn't face it. I ducked into the bathroom, feeling like a ninny. Anyone could come in and find me hiding here, I thought, and then I'd look even more squirrelly and pathetic. I counted to ten, then twenty. At fifty I made myself open the door, leave, walk down the hall, turn right, go into the cafeteria.

There in line were Renée and Maya—together! Amen! Renée must have done all the apologizing about the party and Darcy's phone calls, and I could just slip in with it all taken care of. Good old Renée. Thank God she didn't believe I'd called her an elephant to be mean!

So I went up and joined them as if everything were normal, normal, normal. We pushed our lunch trays down the row, each taking an apple. I didn't think I'd be able to eat it, though. Maya took a glob of egg salad on lettuce, so I did too, then Renée.

"We'll be twins on the inside," I said, and the girls smiled. We all took Jell-O. I hate Jell-O, but it was the principle of the thing.

We got out of line and stood there. We'd been eating at the table under the window forever. None of us said anything, we just moved to the closest table that had room for the three of us and sat down.

We had to talk about *something*, so I told Maya that Candace and Darcy were mad at me too.

"Why?" Maya asked.

Renée answered, "They think they're sticking up for um, sticking up for me! They *say* it's, um, because Brianna called me an, um . . ."

"Elephant," I said, finishing her sentence.

Then Renée started to laugh. "Darcy and Candace are such loyal friends!" she sputtered.

That *was* funny. I laughed too.

"Are they mad at you, Renée?" Maya asked.

So Maya was wondering why Renée was sitting with us and not with Darcy and Candace. I'd wondered too. As far as I knew, she didn't *have* to sit with us.

Renée shrugged. "They're probably, um. They're probably mad at me by now!"

I sneaked a peek at our old table. Who was that with Candace and Darcy? Was it Nicole? I couldn't see her face, but there was no mistaking that red braid. Nicole was in one of my classes, but I didn't really know her.

That's when I realized I wasn't sorry that I wasn't over there at the table by the window. I wouldn't have to worry all the time anymore about getting it right, about fitting in, about keeping my cool through Candace's prickly games or Darcy's cruel comments. No more trying to be who Candace and Darcy wanted me to be.

Just then Darcy stalked toward us. I don't know what Renée did, but Maya hunched up her shoulders, looked down at her plate, and began biting her nails. I tried to look the other way, but my eyes were glued to Darcy, like those soon-to-be victims in scary movies who freeze, watching some horrid creature come right at them. Within seconds Darcy was standing over us.

"Sorry for not inviting you to my sleep-over, Maya," Darcy said, but she sure didn't _look_ sorry. She looked crazy! She was sort of sneering off into space, but her hands and face were shaking, as if she were scared to death. "And I apologize for calling you that night. Tell your mom I apologized," she added flatly. Then she turned around and marched back to the table by the window, march, march, march.

"What was _that?_" Renée asked.

"Tell my _mom?_" Maya asked back, totally confused.

We all looked at one another. Then I started to gig-
gle, and once I started, I couldn't stop. I tried to catch
my breath. Renée and Maya were grinning at me,
wanting to know the joke, waiting to laugh too. Finally
I sputtered out, "The spell is broken!"

My friends wrinkled their foreheads, still wondering
what I meant.

"We're frogs kissed by a princess!" I laughed. "No,
we're sleeping beauties kissed by the prince! Ding-
dong, the witch is dead! We're free!"

Maya

BRIANNA WAS LAUGHING at Darcy, not at me. And she was right! We were free now! Then Renée and I caught Brianna's giggles. I was so glad that we were laughing together that I practically jumped up and hugged them. Instead, when we'd all calmed down, I took a roll of breath mints out of my pocket, popped one in my mouth, and offered them to the girls.

They looked a little embarrassed, but they each took one.

"No hard feelings," I said.

From the way they smiled, I knew everything was going to be all right.

When we got up to leave the lunchroom, my legs were wobbly, exactly like the sensation I'd had Saturday, stepping off of the roller coasters at Magic Moun-tain. But those rides had been nothing compared with this one. I hoped I'd *never*, ever have to take another ride like this again in my life. But I decided to worry about that some other time. For now, I was safe. YA–HOO!

nicole

EVERYONE IN THE CAFETERIA could see me sitting with Candace Newman. I could feel all their eyes on me, and it felt fantastic! But I kept cool. At least I tried to.

And it turned out that Candace was easy to talk to! I'd always wanted to get to know her. And if I'd known how really friendly and sweet she was, I would have talked to her long ago. Funny how I'd always thought that really popular girls were snobs. I'd been totally and completely wrong.

Anyway, Candace and I were sharing our lunches when Candace's sidekick, Darcy, said something about having to apologize to Maya and being grounded or something. And right in the middle of lunch, she got up and went over to those other girls' table.

As soon as she was gone, Candace whispered, "Darcy is really a dear, and I'd hate to hurt her feelings, but she's like a piece of toilet paper stuck to my shoe." Candace shook her leg. I leaned over and pretended to peel an icky bit of toilet paper off her foot. We both wrinkled up our noses and laughed. I really liked Candace. She was so funny!

It was easy to see how Darcy would drive her nuts. The way she looked at Candace was like Sniffo, my dog, when he begged at the table. Ears back, eyes all hopeful. When Sniffo did that, it was cute. When Darcy did that, it creeped me out.

And the way Darcy so *obviously* worshiped Candace! I mean, it was embarrassing to watch. I'd always admired Candace myself. And it was nice, very, very nice, that we were finally getting together, but I'd never in a million years fawn all over her the way Darcy did.

"I feel bad for her, though," Candace said, nodding toward Darcy. "She's kind of delicate emotionally. This is an absolute secret, so promise you won't tell a soul, but Darcy wore Pull-ups, you know, those diaper things for bed wetters? Until she was, like, nine or something!"

Candace's forehead was creased with sympathy. I guess it was sweet of her to be concerned about Darcy's problem. But it didn't seem fair that Candace was being punished just for being too nice. You're supposed to be friends with someone because you *like* them, not because you *pity* them.

Well, I told myself, I was going to change all that. I'd help Candace flick that Darcy off her shoe and show her what *real* friendship is like. Candace, of all people, deserved it.